DANGEROUS

WOLF RANCH
BOOK 10

RENEE ROSE

VANESSA VALE

Pack Rule #10 –
Keep control of your inner wolf.

I live alone on the mountain for a reason.
I'm dangerous—too strong, too aggressive, too close to
feral.
But then *she* shows up—with sweet curves, sultry
voice, and a scent that drives my wolf insane.
A gorgeous human, pouring drinks at Cody's Saloon
and hiding a shattered past behind her smile.
I know the second I scent her—she's mine. My mate.
The one I was made for.
My wolf surges to claim her. But she's just escaped a
controlling ex who tried to silence her music, her
voice, her very soul. My alpha instincts are everything
she fears–I'm possessive. Dominant. Overwhelming.
And she's terrified of losing her freedom again.
I've held back my entire life. From the pack. From
power. From the madness in my blood.
But I won't hold back from her. Not when she's what
anchors me.
I'll protect her. Please her. Put her music back in the
world.
And if she'll let me, I'll make her mine—completely.
Even if I have to unleash every dark, dangerous part of
myself to do it.

1

BOONE

*S*HE WAS HERE.

A scent in the throng activated my wolf. The delicious female scent had notes of honey and peaches. I never knew I liked them until now.

Mate.

I'd heard I was supposed to know the moment I scented my mate, but it was hard to conceive how that would feel. How amazing it was. And frustrating. I'd never felt it myself. Never imagined it since I'd lived so many years in a big city. Ironic, since there were so many people in comparison to Cooper Valley.

Now I knew. It felt like a switch turned on and there was no way to turn it back off.

My brain told me it made no sense. Nothing got between a shifter and his mate, including logic and reason. She was mine, wherever she was.

My breath rushed into my lungs in a huge gulp, and my blood traveled south to my dick.

Fuck me. I was instantly hard because of a scent.

Because of a mate I had never even laid eyes on. Thank fuck, I'd come down the mountain to drop off that load of firewood for Cody at his cabin, which forced me, the fucker, to come to the bar to get his payment in person.

Where was she?

Who was she?

I scanned the crowd, a hunter after his prey. I was sure my eyes changed color, sharpened like it usually did when my wolf became dominant. My nose zeroed in on that honey scent, but a Saturday crowd packed into Cody's Saloon made it really hard to distinguish where it came from.

Where was she?

Females swayed to the rhythm of the country music, all decked out in their skimpy look-at-me outfits, despite the cold weather and piles of snow outside. Even more males packed in all around them, dancing closer, hoping to get lucky by the end of the night. Many of them would. Hopefully, I would, too.

Except their get-laid goals meant nothing to me

and my wolf. They'd better get out of the fucking way because one of these females in here belonged to me.

I moved through the cluster of bodies, trying to trace the scent. The jolt I'd felt when I caught it the first time nearly made me shift right here in Cody's, surrounded by a bunch of humans who would freak the fuck out.

I was thirty-eight. Fuck–I'd given up on finding my mate the second I left town to go to college. Yeah, me at Columbia University. At sixteen. I'd grown into my size by then and had refused to even consider a fight with Rob Wolf for alpha when his father died. I'd almost killed my father in that argument and had run–tail between my legs–as far as I could go from pack land to The Big Apple and college.

It had been safer for everyone with me gone, shifter or human, because I was a surly fucker even when I was feeling friendly. Except, years later, I also left New York City just as fast as I had Cooper Valley. I'd gone from fancy hedge fund manager to lumberjack recluse because it seemed no matter where I lived or what I did, I was bad news. I spent my days up in the woods. I chopped down trees for a living. I didn't have coworkers for a reason. No watercooler talk. Hell, I was rusty at socializing, and this visit into town made it obvious. Except now I was obsessed with finding the one person I'd spend the rest of my life with.

Her.

With the memory of her scent permanently embedded in my frontal lobe, I was nearly feral. I felt my canines start to drop, ready to find, bite, and fuck.

If I didn't find her and mark her soon, I could lose control, and that would be a bad thing. Staying up at my cabin wouldn't keep me or anyone else safe any longer. I'd slowly go crazy and eventually moon mad.

I had to find her. I had to have her. I had to make her mine. Or I'd need to be put down.

I skirted the dance floor along the perimeter but couldn't find the scent again.

I wasn't a dancer. Hell, I didn't really even like people, especially not crowds. Fuck it. I elbowed my way right through the center like a charging bull. I was a full head and shoulders taller than almost everyone in the place, even the guys wearing Stetsons, and the intensity of my need to find my female made me aggressive. As if they sensed the danger they were in, the crowd parted and made way for me.

Still, no mate.

Where the FUCK was she?

I sent a frantic glance toward the door. What if she'd been on her way out, and her scent still lingered, but she was gone? What if I fucking *missed* my mate? What if she was out there right now, never for me to find?

I growled, the deep rumble in my chest heard over the music by those nearby.

I slammed back through the dance floor in the other direction, not caring if I bumped people out of my way, stalking through the main area of the bar toward the front door.

Cody caught my scowl as I passed him behind the bar and raised a quizzical brow, but I ignored it and him. I wasn't going to make problems for him or any of his patrons, if that was what he was thinking–at least as long as they stayed out of my way.

I just needed my mate. Now.

I threw the door open and stalked out on the sidewalk. I'd be able to smell her better out there, with fewer scents to confuse things.

I lifted my nose in the cold air. It was dark, the streetlights giving everything an extra white glow, making the piles of snow at the curb even brighter.

No. She hadn't been here recently.

It had snowed a foot the night before, but the sidewalk was dry and clear. I should have been cold but... no. My blood ran hot. Too hot. Especially now.

I stepped back inside where the space was cramped and suddenly extra stuffy. I scanned the big room once more. She wasn't on the dance floor. Or by the mechanical bull. Or at the bar.

If she wasn't in this area then... the bathroom?

I clomped back around the high-top tables, bumping into Rand, a wolf friend of mine.

"Hey, Boone. Really good to see you. You came down off the mountain!" He slapped me on the shoulder and looked equally pleased and stunned. I didn't show my face in town for anything more than groceries or other required appointments, and those were few and far between. "Natalie and I are sure liking the new bed."

"Yeah," I muttered, passing right by him to head back toward the bathrooms and storeroom.

He and his new wife Natalie, a human, wanted something special, so I'd found the perfect tree, chopped it down, and gave it to my brother, Roy, to do his carpentry magic and turn it into their bed. I chopped. He built. Everyone bought.

"Okay, nice talkin' to you," he called after me with a laugh. We'd known each other for years, and thankfully, he didn't take offense at my rudeness. I knew I was rude. I just didn't care.

When I explained why I was acting like more of a jackass than usual, he'd understand.

Toward the back of the building, her scent grew stronger. Yes!

Something in me both relaxed and grew more agitated at the same time. My dick stirred, my wolf prowled, eager.

Mate.

Mine.

Claim.

I sucked a deep breath in through my nostrils to calm down, but it backfired, since I got more of her honey scent. Fuck, that smelled so fucking good.

I'm coming for you, mate.

I almost shifted again. A dog-like shiver rippled through my body as I tried to get control. Any human eyeing me would think I was chilled. My canines were already lengthening further, like my wolf was gonna mark her the second she came out of the ladies' room.

That probably wouldn't be my best move. It was done–I'd heard of females who got marked in the middle of the mating games, the moment their mate found them–but I should try to show more finesse.

Buy her a drink first.

Flirt a little.

Ha! Me. Finesse and flirting weren't two of my qualities. Hell, I was shit at both.

I was more the "take her home, fuck her thoroughly, and sink my teeth into her sweet honey flesh" kind of shifter male. Or beat the shit out of your own father and leave him for dead kind of shifter male. Either way, I had no clue what the fuck I was doing, especially with a female, only driven by my wolf.

I attempted to be casual, leaning my back

against the white wall next to the ladies' room and stared at a framed historical photo. I helped Cody install the wood wainscotting here when he updated the saloon a few years ago. Chopped the pine and hewed it myself from the woods surrounding Wolf Ranch to make the trim and the flooring, even finding some recycled wood planks for accents and trim.

It seemed fitting that I'd find my mate right here, in my pack mate's bar, after living in New York. That my home was hers.

I tapped my leather boot on the floor with impatience. She wasn't coming out. How long did women take in the bathroom, anyway? What was there to do besides take a piss and wash your hands?

A few women had gone in and come out while I waited, but my mate hadn't emerged.

A spike of aggression snarled through me as the idea of missing her once again returned. Before I could think or dial it back, I lifted my meaty arm and pounded on the door then pushed it wide and stomped in.

"What the fuck? Get out!" A woman putting on lipstick in front of the mirror glared at me, then her eyes widened when she took an extra second to really look me over. I was big, really fucking big, and it made her think twice about snapping at me. I hated the way I was looked at. Like I was truly feral. Like she was afraid I might hurt her.

I wouldn't harm her or any woman, but she didn't know that. Especially when I was on the hunt for my fucking mate.

I ignored her because she sure as hell wasn't my mate, lifted my nose, and sniffed.

Fuck! She wasn't in here!

I spun on my heel and strode back down the hall just as a petite blonde cocktail server came out from behind the bar with a tray stacked with Bud Lite and Mountain Man Scotch Ale bottles. The scent of beer hit me first, then I caught the scent of her sweetness.

It was her! Holy hell, she was so fucking perfect. Tiny. Everyone was tiny compared to me. She probably came up to my shoulder, and her waist was the same thickness as my thigh. Shit, she was fragile. Breakable. Her hair followed her jawline and her bangs were a fringe over her forehead. It was the prettiest shade of honey blonde to match her scent. And blue eyes that were a pretty contrast to her hair. Her mouth was narrow, but full, and when she smiled at a customer... I wanted that aimed at me and no one else.

In fact, I wanted to go over there and rip the guy's head off who she was chatting with. I doubted he was asking for her number while he tapped the credit card machine to pay.

Hell, he better not. It didn't matter. Those smiles would be all for me soon enough.

I licked my lips because in her bar T-shirt and jeans, I couldn't miss her curves. Proportioned, but no question I'd be able to cup a tit in my palm. I could easily span her waist with my two huge, dinner plate-sized hands. I'd–

"Whoa, there," I said when she was about to go past me.

I shot forward, taking the tray from her with one hand as I looped my free arm around her waist and pulled her body up against mine. Yup, fucking tiny. But soft. Warm. Fragrant.

She gasped when her soft ass hit my hard thighs. My canines lengthened, and every muscle in my body trembled like a coil set to spring. I lowered my nose to her silky hair and inhaled deeply.

Fucking heaven.

There was absolutely no question. This was my mate. I had her in my arms. I could toss her over my shoulder. Carry her out of her. Take her to my cabin, mark her, and keep her forever.

Mine. *Mine.* MINE.

"Hey! Let *go!*" she cried.

It took me a second to realize she was struggling to get free, and the rise of her voice wasn't her screaming from an orgasm but from panic. Of course, she would panic at being grabbed by a rough-and-tumble guy like me. Hell, I'd punch any asshole in this place who did the same to her.

Fuck. I immediately let her loose. As she whirled to face me, I caught the scent of both anger and fear on her.

That was when I realized something else from her scent. Something I should have noticed first–she was human.

My mate was human.

Holy hell.

That made her even more fragile. More breakable. I was huge. I could hurt her. Damage her perfection. I'd have to be careful. Hold myself back. Protect her.

Shit. I basically just assaulted a human female who didn't know what the fuck was wrong with me. She couldn't recognize me by scent like a she-wolf.

Didn't understand my claim or why I grabbed her.

She probably thought I was a low-life jerk who felt entitled to be handsy with the waitresses.

I blinked my eyes, realizing they probably changed color and were showing my wolf.

"Sorry." I held my free hand up in front of me.

Her face, which had gone pale, now flushed with color as her gaze took the long trip up and down my huge body. Surprising the hell out of me, she didn't panic. Or run away screaming.

Thank fuck, to that.

She stood and looked her fill and... did she like what she saw? Fuck, I hoped so. I'd never had so much self doubt as I did in this moment.

She cocked a hip, pretending to be a badass, but her finger trembled when she pointed it at the tray of beer in my hand. Fire. I loved it. She might be tiny, but she wasn't weak. "Give it back."

My mind raced to think of an excuse. Something to explain why I'd just grabbed her and took her tray. It was so fucking obvious. I had zero fucking finesse. I'd fucked things up from the first second I found her.

"I'm sorry, I uh, thought you were someone else." I tried to keep the growl from my voice because that was the biggest fucking lie. I knew, for the first time and with absolute certainty, she was exactly the person I'd been looking for my entire life.

No—dammit! That was an idiotic thing to say. Now she'd think I was a player. Or had a girlfriend. Or grabbed only specific women to manhandle.

I shook my head and remembered *flirting and finesse*. I sighed. "That's not what I meant. I just, ah... honestly?" –I shoved my fingers through my hair which gave away my anxiety– "I took one look at you and had to have you."

There. That was better. Romantic, even. Human females were all about romance.

Her head tipped back to meet my gaze–I was that much taller, not because she was small but because I was fucking huge. Her brows drew together, and her gorgeous blue eyes narrowed at me.

Okay, flirting didn't seem to work.

Fate, I wanted to touch her again. I needed to get her out of this crowded bar and alone.

Her bowtie lips drew together in a tight line. "Get used to disappointment," she snapped and set her hand on her hip. She had sass, too. Fuck, yes. "The tray?"

The tray. What tray? I followed her gaze to my hand where her cocktail tray was still balanced. Oh–fuck! Well, at least I hadn't dumped the drinks in my frenzy to get her scent into my nostrils.

"I'll carry it for you," I said over a whoop in the crowd when a popular song started. I leaned down, so she could hear me since she wasn't a fucking shifter with wolf ears and amazing hearing. "Where were you headed?"

When she realized I was serious, she looked over her shoulder to Cody behind the bar.

Fuck. She thought she needed help. To get away from *me*.

Her mate.

How much more could I fuck up?

I racked my brain for something to say to fix this.

Dealing with people–shifter or human–wasn't my speciality. I wasn't a people person. I was a tree person. A nature person. A mountain man.

I could never have been an alpha of the Wolf pack like my cousin, Rob, no matter what my father had wanted. I lived up on the mountain high above Cooper Valley and the rest of the pack for a reason. Far from people and embarrassing situations like this. It also kept people safe from my recklessness. I could be dangerous.

I gave my best attempt at charming, even tried to smile. "I'll trade you the tray for your name."

She rolled her eyes like this was the third time tonight she'd heard something similar. While I didn't want to have to prove myself to her because she was fucking mine, I liked knowing she didn't let any guy mess with her.

Cody came down the length of the bar toward us. Set his hands on the hard, glossy surface, and said, "Thanks for bringing down that cut wood. My pile for the stove is getting low. I– what's going on, Boone?"

Thank fuck, I found my mate here in a bar owned by a fellow shifter and pack member than the grocery store where she might fling canned goods at me.

"I..." I had to concede I needed help. Maybe Cody could throw me a lifeline.

"You workin' here now?" he asked, when I stumbled with my words. "If not, hand the tray off. I've got thirsty customers," he instructed with a smirk. I was glad of it because I needed to be told what to do here. I offered the tray to my mate, relishing the way our fingers brushed when she took it.

As she turned and sped off into the crowd without even a backward glance–which was fucking shitty because she didn't have any qualms about walking away from her mate–I worried about her. I couldn't protect her if I couldn't see her in this zoo. But Cody wouldn't let her–or any woman–work here if he thought she was in any kind of danger.

So I focused on Cody instead of going after her. It took some effort to make my mouth work properly as I set my forearms on the bar and admitted, "She's....my..."

"Mate," Cody finished for me flatly. He pointed to one of his eyes then mine. "Holy shit, yeah, your wolf is showing."

He grinned, and I dropped my head between my shoulders, blinked a couple of times, trying unsuccessfully to get my wolf on a leash. That was going to be an impossible task for the foreseeable future. "I need her," I rasped when I looked up again.

I was feeling fucking desperate since she walked away. Like I was going to shift and tear this place apart if I didn't get her back in my arms in the next ten seconds. My heart rate was up, my blood pressure must've been through the roof. My fists were clenched. My dick throbbed. My wolf prowled and howled with frustration.

I was losing my shit.

Cody shook his head. He reached across the bar and put his hand firmly on my shoulder. Squeezed. He met my gaze with a serious one of his own. "That's too fucking bad, Boone. You can't have her."

2

SUMMER

My knees wobbled as I cut through the crowd to deliver the beers. My hands shook, and I tried not to spill and make a mess like it was my first day on the job.

Jeez, that guy was huge. His hands were the size of baseball mitts, and his thickly muscled arm felt like a steel cable wrapped around me. He smelled of pine and mountain air and growled like a bear. He sure was as big as one.

I wouldn't call myself gorgeous, but guys hit on me all the time, especially working here at Cody's. Maybe they were hoping to score with someone they thought was easy… a waitress. This guy was different. More. Not just his size, but his presence and his energy was bigger. That made me immediately wonder whether he was bigger *everywhere.*

I was a mix of turned on and terrified because why on earth was my mind going *there*?

Lordy, my nipples were hard and chafing against my bra, which made no sense at all.

I couldn't believe he saw me walking by and grabbed me as if I belonged to him! The *nerve.* The arrogance of these alpha males.

He was just like Marty–acting like women were a possession that could just be acquired. A collectible that he wasn't going to share with anyone. Like he had me. Grabbed and kept. Something to put up high on a shelf away from others.

I took one look at you and had to have you.

Not a great pickup line, buddy. It also immediately made my mind stir up thoughts of Marty because he'd said something similar to me when we first met all those years ago. I'd been dumb then, buying it. I was wiser now.

Although in this big guy's defense, he probably didn't need to use pickup lines. I'd bet most women looked at the hot, bearded lumberjack and waved their panties in surrender. Before Marty, I might have been tempted because any conscious woman would find him panty-melting.

But now I knew how jealous and possessive guys like that could be. They thought you belonged to them. A possession. They needed to control you. *Own* you. They were crafty about luring you into their trap, and once you were caught, they made sure you lost all your friends and resources to fight back when they eventually got violent.

Gaslighting was their specialty. Plus, isolating and separating from loved ones and friends. Making me doubt myself with everything I said, everything I did, and God, like now, everything I thought.

Had I done something special to draw his attention? Was it my fault because I wore–

NO! I had to stop thinking that. I hadn't done anything wrong, and he'd wrapped an arm around me.

A shiver went down my spine imagining if a guy *his* size got violent. There'd be no walking away from it. I'd be dead, just like I would have been if I hadn't gotten away from Marty when I did.

I delivered the drinks on my tray and took new orders, all with a shaky, pasted-on smile, my heart still jack-hammering in my chest.

I was safe here. Cody, the owner, knew him. Called him Boone.

Plus, Natalie and Rand were here tonight. I'd spotted them in the crowd and waved although they'd ended up in another waitress's section. They wouldn't let anything happen to me either. I knew *Rand* wouldn't.

I took a deep breath. Let it out. Then another.

I was safe. Totally safe. *Safe.*

Marty wasn't here. This guy? While he wasn't Marty, I didn't know him at all.

As I headed back to the bar, my tray stacked with a few empties I found on the way, I couldn't help but scan for the big man–Boone. Not because I was interested. Not because I was afraid.

Just because I couldn't stop thinking about him, how his big arm had been warm and strong around me. How his rumbly voice had made my panties damp–yeah, it was difficult to admit that I was drawn to him and that my body had responded so quickly. That in itself was a surprise because I pretty much thought my libido got crushed by Marty. I hadn't felt an inkling of arousal for a long time and now... out of the blue for Mr. Lumberjack?

I'd told him to let go, and he had. Immediately. Even apologized.

He was different from Marty because he hadn't blamed his actions on whether I was dressed sluttily, and he couldn't help himself. If my lipstick was too bright or it'd looked like I flirted with a customer.

Now that I'd calmed down, separated out that this guy wasn't Marty–it was pretty obvious physically since Marty was a half foot shorter and probably a hundred pounds lighter–and reminded myself my ex was in a different time zone, I wanted to get a better look at his face. Because what I remembered was worth a second look. He was that handsome.

There. My heart started hammering when I scanned the room and saw him again. He stood at the cocktail station where I went to empty my tray and give Cody the new orders. I braced myself as I walked up for his fresh attempt to "seduce" me or whatever it was he thought he was doing, but he said nothing.

He remained still–like, statue-still–and watched me. I felt his gaze on me but nothing more.

As I did my thing, collecting cocktail napkins and straws, pretending I didn't notice a handsome bearded behemoth wasn't beside me, it occurred to me that his stillness might have been intended to soothe me. Like the way one moved slowly dealing with a skittish horse. That instead of freaking me out in his presence, he silently wanted me to know that I was safe with him.

Or was it him trying to lull me into a sense of security?

I knew what that was like, too. Put your guard down and then–

"Summer!" My boss beckoned me over while his hands moved quickly, pouring drinks for patrons three deep at the bar. His young wife, Riley, sat in front of him with friends her age, looking like she was having a great time. She was a few years younger than me, and there was no question Cody was smitten. While he tended to the customers, I saw him looking her way often enough.

I smiled at her as I approached and placed the ticket with my new drink orders on the bar before Cody, so he could make them next.

"I'm sorry Boone scared you," he said as he shook the cocktail shaker then poured a chilled martini into a glass, garnishing it with an olive-laden toothpick. While most people here ordered beer or shots, occasionally a fancier drink was requested. I did know that he didn't make anything with little drink umbrellas. Bar rules.

"He lives up on the mountain, and his manners must've gotten rusty."

I glanced over at Boone. In the sea of people weaving, talking, or laughing around him, he appeared to be frozen in time. Like he'd been left out in the winter weather and turned to ice. Where he might have been frozen, I was heated looking his way. He was that attractive. One word? Rugged.

His hair was trimmed short on the sides and longer on the top, and his beard, while full, was equally groomed. His shoulders had to take up an entire doorway, and his flannel stretched taut over the expanse. I knew because I came up to his chest and eyed one of the buttons. He wore jeans that were worn and molded to him in ways Marty could never carry off.

"I want you to know–Boone's perfectly safe," Colt added, leaning my way as he set four shots of tequila on my tray. "I vouch for him one hundred percent." Even though he was crazy busy, he stopped, tipped his chin down, and met my gaze. Held it. I didn't see a lie there. He'd never treated me poorly, never lied to me. Never called me names like *honey* or *sweetheart*. He'd never given me a reason not to trust him.

"Okay."

If he said that Boone was safe, then that meant *Boone,* the hulking giant, was safe. Something clicked inside me. Like the very sturdy concrete dam I put up between the part of me that had been instantly attracted to Boone and the part that said "no way" to another overbearing jerk just broke. Heat pooled between my legs because I was drawn to him. Because I got the green light from Cody.

I had no idea why I was attracted to a guy who was

so big and growly that he could snap me like a twig. Marty hadn't been this size, far from it, and that meant my instincts were terrible.

But... Cody was a bar owner. Saw lots of men trying every angle possible to get in a girl's panties. He wasn't a beer-goggling drunk girl who thought Boone was hot. His judgment wasn't tainted by desire. The only interest I ever saw in his gaze was directed toward Riley.

I sneaked another peek at the giant man. What would it be like to be with such a virile specimen of manhood? He was as big as a tree. I could *climb* him like a tree.

That thought made my nipples even harder.

It had been years since anything had turned me on—I'd shut the sexual part of myself off with all the bullshit Marty put me through. Something about Boone made me come alive again. Like turning on a faucet or flipping a switch. Made me *feel.*

My desire went from off to ON. My panties were ruined.

But that felt dangerous, too. Instant need was scary. That was how it started with Marty. He'd seemed charming. Confident. Capable. Attractive in a clean-cut, I'm-not-remotely-dangerous way. He was a cop! I should have felt safest with him. He'd lured me in and put a ring on my finger, and before I knew it, the real

Marty came out, and I was trapped with a whole police force standing behind him.

Cody rapped his knuckles on the bar top. "If you wanted something from him–"

My gaze whipped up to meet his at those words.

"–but felt nervous after what you've been through, I assure you that he'd follow any rule you set for him."

Any rule I set for him?

Wait–*if I wanted something?*

I licked my lips. Was Cody literally suggesting I have a one night stand or a fling with Boone? That it would be okay, that I'd be safe, and that I'd... what? Set the rules about what we did and how we did it?

Did I want something? Could I feel that way again? Could I act on sex in such an easy, fun way like I'd seen women do multiple times already tonight. Want a guy? They went for it.

God, he was. Cody was blatantly suggesting I *use* this guy. For *sex*, I presumed. Or, I guessed, I could use him to move a load of lumber. Pick up a piano. Bench press a car.

He seemed pretty capable of anything physical I could ask of him.

Did I want sex with that big, burly man?

His arm around my waist had been the first time a man besides Marty had ever touched me. My father hadn't been a hugger. Marty wasn't a hugger either, but he'd touched me. Oh, he had.

Boone's touch was possessive, and that was what scared me, but it also felt... protective. Different. Like those big muscles weren't going to be used against me but would protect me and take care of me.

Keep me safe.

I licked my lips and wondered. Could I let a guy like Boone touch me? Did I want that? To feel his calloused palms coast over my skin? The soft feel of his whiskers on my inner thighs? To feel the thick heft of his dick as he pressed into me?

I squirmed where I stood at those very naughty ideas. Suddenly, the bar was stifling hot. I wanted to go outside and drop into the snow and make snow angels to cool off.

Did I want Boone? I looked up at the man in question. Yes. Yes, I did.

Cody's suggestion that I could give that clearly dominant man rules meant while he was definitely the bigger of the two of us, I would be in charge.

I snagged the beer bottles I needed and popped their caps off, loading them onto my tray, then added the shot of whisky, vodka tonic, and whisky sour that Cody had poured for me.

I wanted to grab that shot and down it myself. I needed some liquid courage. I could do this. I could be a normal woman with needs. Needs Boone could fill, no question.

When I strode back out from behind the bar, I stopped in front of my new admirer, who'd watched me approach with his very intense dark eyes. Dark eyes that hadn't left me since I arrived at the bar.

"My name is Summer." I pointed my finger right up in his face. I was going to do this. "First rule–no touching without asking permission."

3

───────

BOONE

Hell, yeah.

She gave me her name. Gave me a rule.

Like all shifters, I had remarkably powerful hearing, but the bar was packed. And loud. Cody must've said something to her to vouch for me. I owed him big time. But fuck, my wolf nearly tore free from me and howled when he'd told me she was married.

Married! Claimed by another human by their legalities that didn't mean anything to shifters.

He'd said she was married, but divorce papers had been filed. That there wasn't a chance she was going back to the man. Cody said she was actually staying over at Rand and Natalie's place next to Wolf Ranch. I had to admit, it eased my mind she was under that roof where she'd be protected by a pack member.

"Summer." It came out as a grunt, but I loved having her name in my mouth. Fuck, I sounded like a big oaf instead of a guy with the MBA and a big Wall Street career under his belt.

My mate's name was Summer, like the most glorious season of the year in Montana. It was as beautiful as she was.

I extended my palm but laid it open on the bar rather than handshake style, still trying to show her I was harmless–a decided challenge for a guy who was six feet seven inches and two hundred and fifty pounds.

And waited. As long as she was in front of me, I could wait all night.

She studied it for a moment then lowered her tray to the counter. I couldn't miss her hand shake as she placed it in mine. Her eyes were grey-blue, like the sky before a storm, and something in her slender stature and the firm set of her chest made me think she'd been through a lot.

Maybe the divorce had been hard on her.

Fuck, I hoped she wasn't heartbroken. Had she loved the man? Dumbass, she'd married him–of course, they'd been in love. Yet she was eyeing me with definite hesitance but also interest. I knew it. My wolf knew it. I could *scent* it. That honey sweetness was stronger now.

Whatever her deal was, I could work with it.

I *had* to.

She was mine. I needed her in order to survive.

Shit. I was smart. Really fucking smart, but if I didn't figure out how to win her over so I could claim her, I'd lose control of my wolf. I was barely hanging onto my wolf's leash as it was, and it'd only been a few minutes.

This was more than just surviving though. Her being my mate wasn't just a way to keep from going moon mad. I wanted her. My heart *and* my dick. I needed to see her smile. To see her come on my cock. To be by her side and take away whatever haunted her. If she suffered, that wouldn't happen again.

Her gentle touch, palm to palm, made the air charge around us like a heated night before a storm. I gently closed my fingers around hers. Her hand looked small and delicate in my large calloused one. Soft, warm. Her nails weren't painted or long, but they were neatly filed and clean.

It struck me again that she was human. Fucking human! That meant she was a fragile glass. Breakable. When she got hurt, she didn't heal instantly.

It made my wolf want to bare his teeth against any

and every danger that came her way. I felt the need to keep her safe more fiercely than ever.

I cleared my throat, as if it was rusty from use. "I won't touch you again without permission," I promised, holding her gaze. Making sure she knew I heard her rule and would follow it.

She searched my face as if trying to decide if I meant it, yet she'd put her palm in mine.

A small step, but it was a fucking step.

I held perfectly still for her scrutiny and let the crowded bar slip away. I didn't hear the twangy music or hear the conversations around us. "Tell me all your rules."

Fuck. Did that sound too gruff? Too bossy? Everything that came out of my mouth sounded growly, like it was my wolf talking. I really didn't know how to flirt and finesse. I hadn't had to in order to make deals with clients, watch the stock market, and learn trends and economic patterns to turn my clients' millions into even more millions in a long fucking time.

But I'd better learn fast.

She blinked. Stared at me. I didn't think she had any other rules logged yet. Hell, we just met. Maybe I'd have to break them first for her to figure out what they were.

I could work with that.

She glanced back out into the crowd and lifted her hand, picking up her tray. She was already moving when she said the words over her shoulder, "Wait here."

"I'm not going anywhere," I swore. Not without my mate. I sure as hell wasn't ever leaving this place without my mate.

I settled on a free stool where I was, tracking her movements in the mirror above the bar. At some point, Cody dropped off a glass of ice water in front of me. Twenty minutes later, Summer sailed back, working quickly to divest her tray of used drinks and bottles.

I let her work. My wolf was impatient, but I held him by the scruff of his neck. I couldn't just throw her over my shoulder and carry her off in the middle of her shift. I couldn't carry her off, period, because I was sure that was one of her rules. She had to walk out of here with me willingly. And, I reminded myself, that was going to take flirting and finesse. Or at least a smile or something that didn't scare her.

Plus, Cody'd lose his shit if I did that.

She refilled her tray with fresh drinks Cody had made then paused in front of me again. Sitting as I was, we were almost eye level. "Rule number two: you have to take no for an answer."

My eyes widened, and I hesitated. My wolf said absolutely not. He would never ever stop trying for her.

But I could see this was important to her. She was

afraid I wouldn't respect her or honor her wishes, and it made me wonder who in the past hadn't listened to her.

Who hadn't stopped when she'd said no.

I bowed my head, leaned in a little, so she could hear me. "I promise I will take no for an answer."

Even if it killed me.

And it *might* fucking kill me if she told me no to being together entirely.

Cody flicked the lights to show last call, and the energy in the saloon got even more frenzied as everyone rushed to get their last drink and find their hook-up for the night. I stayed in my seat watching my mate in the mirror through all of this, biding my time.

Thirty minutes later, Cody turned off the music and illuminated the overhead fluorescent lights to signal that the bar was closed, and it was time for everyone to clear out. The customers squinted their eyes at the glare, scurrying to get out of the harsh light.

I held my position at the end of the bar until the place was empty. My ears rang from the sudden quiet. Cody wouldn't kick me out, and I wasn't leaving without my mate. His own mate had left right before last call–I'd seen Cody carry her out to her car before he returned to finish up. He'd come back with a smile on his face, and I knew it wasn't only some of his customers who were gonna get lucky tonight.

I just hoped I could figure out how to convince Summer that I'd make her the luckiest woman in the fucking world if she left with me.

After everyone but the employees were gone, I stood from my position and pitched in with the cleanup, helping Summer to bus the dirty glasses and toss the empty bottles into the recycling bin. I picked up and hauled the full recycling container out back, forgetting to make it look heavy. I could get away with showing more strength than most wolves on account of my size. When I came back in, Summer had a large push broom and was sweeping the floor with it.

I gently took it from her hands, waited for her to meet my eyes. "I got this, Summer."

I wanted to touch her. *Desperately.* But still, I bided my time. She was on the clock. The sooner I helped her finish here, the sooner I could ask if I could take her home.

I made quick work of sweeping all the trash from the floor–and damn, there was a lot of trash! I guessed when the lights were low, people didn't think twice about throwing shit underfoot. When I finished, I hauled two full trash barrels out to the dumpster in the back of the lot, one in each hand, and returned to wash up in the bathroom.

When I came back out into the main bar area, my hands damp, there she was.

I stopped two feet from her. Looked down at her. Waited. Waited. Breathed in her sweet scent. *Fucking waited.*

"Okay," she said.

I frowned. "Okay?"

"Okay, I give you permission to touch me."

With a gentle touch, I lifted her up onto the bar–fuck, was she light–so we were eye to eye. Setting my hands on her knees, I parted them and stepped between.

Her eyes were wide with surprise, not fear.

I cupped her face, sliding my calloused thumbs over her silky cheeks. Then leaned in and kissed her.

4

SUMMER

Wow. WOW.

I'd never been kissed like this. Equal parts reverent and fierce. Boone's mouth was soft, but his kiss potent. I gasped, and his tongue found mine. Tangled.

Lush licks, gentle angling of my head where he wanted me, our mouths mated. God, his tongue was thrusting in my mouth like I imagined his cock would my pussy.

If he could kiss my lips like this, I wondered what he could do lower with his head between my thighs. I'd heard of beard burn being a thing, but it was happening. My pussy clenched in anticipation.

I hooked my heels into his butt and pulled him

closer. Felt the heat radiate off him. Breathed in his scent. Like woods and pine and clean soap.

His hands slid down to my neck, cupped me there, then lower to my shoulders, then down my arms, as if learning me, all the while his mouth was on mine.

The initial surprise was gone, and need took over. My fingers tangled in his soft flannel and gripped, afraid I'd float away if I didn't hang on. Afraid he'd stop. His body was hard. Muscular. Sturdy.

"Boone," I whispered, when he kissed along my jaw to right behind my ear. His beard was soft against my skin.

Oh. That spot made me shiver.

I tilted my head, lifted my hips off the bar to rub against him. I'd never been so aroused in my life. Not in all the years I'd been married. Not ever. And Boone and I had all our clothes on and–

A throat cleared. Then again.

It wasn't me. It wasn't Boone.

We weren't alone. Oh my God! So embarrassing!

I gasped, and Boone pulled back. An inch.

"You gonna have sex on my bar?"

Cody.

Holy hell. I was making out on top of my boss's bar. *On top.*

I felt Boone's chest rumble beneath my knuckles where I *still* held on to him. Then he pulled back, but he ignored Cody. His eyes met mine. Held. They were lighter than I remembered, but no less intense. His cheeks were flushed beneath his beard, his lips red and slick.

"You want me to make you come here or at your place?" he asked.

Oh my. While it was a question, the orgasm was a given. I just had to decide where I was going to get it. It also meant he didn't care about the sanitary standards of the bar top or if Cody watched. He wanted me that badly.

I bit my lip, trying not to laugh and die of embarrassment at the same time. "My place."

Cody, who seemed to have somehow heard my whisper, called, "Have fun, you two."

Have fun. *Have fun.*

It was all I could think about as I drove to my little apartment above my friend Natalie's garage, Boone following. His headlights were a constant the whole way, but so was my clit pulsing and my nipples throbbing.

Natalie's husband, Rand, was a contractor and had designed and built the accessory building to match the style of the rebuilt farmhouse. From what Natalie had shared, the original house had burned down in a fire after she moved in, set by some guy who didn't like the idea of her running a bed and breakfast, which had been her original plan when she inherited the place. The two buildings were connected by a glassed-in breezeway and far enough apart that I didn't feel like moving in meant crowding the newlyweds.

Beneath my apartment, the garage had four stalls, big enough for their personal vehicles, and an old truck with a plow on the front to handle clearing their long driveway of the constant Montana snow. They also had ATVs and Rand's tool trailer.

My space was one big room with a bathroom, a kitchenette, sofa, and bed. Windows looked out on the back of the snow-covered ranch and made me wonder if winter would ever end.

Fleeing my marriage, I'd run here to stay with my friend, far from Los Angeles to start over. To learn who I was, what I wanted.

Tonight, what I wanted was Boone.

He stood just inside the entry to my apartment, winter cap in hand. Watching me. Waiting.

I unzipped my heavy winter coat, but his voice–and the words–made my hands still.

"Let me," he said. His voice was deep and rumbly, like a rockslide.

I let my hands fall to my side as he leaned down and unzipped my jacket, pushed it off my shoulders. He hung it on the hook by the door.

I swallowed, wondering if I'd turned the heat up

too high. I wondered if he could hear my heart pounding.

He dropped to one knee with a heavy thud, and we were now eye to eye then patted his thigh.

"Put your foot here," he instructed.

Settling my hands on his shoulders for balance, I did as asked. Not breaking eye contact, he tugged off my shoe, then I put my foot down and switched.

He patted his thick thigh once more, and I cocked my head.

"Sit."

My mouth twitched, and I sat, feeling the hard play of muscle beneath my thighs. So warm. So big. So–

Oh my.

He kissed me again, but unlike the kiss at the bar that started out slow, this was hot right from the start. Open-mouthed, tongues tangling. As if he'd been thinking about nothing else on the drive here.

Then he stood, taking me with him and carrying me across the room to my bed.

He could have tossed me, but he didn't. He laid me gently on the made bed as if I was fragile, then rose to his towering height.

"Permission to strip you bare and fuck you like you need."

5

———

BOONE

SUMMER'S MOUTH opened and closed because of my words. She also flushed a pretty shade of pink, a pink I imagined matched her nipples and her pussy.

I would treat her with infinite care, but I wasn't a romantic guy. My mouth watered with the taste of her arousal that I could now scent on the air. Sweet honey. As soon as I said *fuck you like you need*, she'd creamed, and no doubt her panties were ruined.

She pushed up onto her elbows. Her bar t-shirt, jeans, and socks were the farthest things from sexy lingerie. Fuck, she'd look gorgeous in lace or silk, no doubt, but I craved her bare. So did my wolf. My mate didn't need anything to make her more alluring.

My cock was already leaking pre-cum, and my balls ached to sink into her. She'd be tight. I knew it.

"Yes. You have permission to do both."

Hooking an ankle, I started with her socks.

"Boone," she said. I lifted my eyes from my task and met hers. "I've, um... it's been a while."

She thought that would be a concern?

I tugged off the sock and let it drop to the floor. "No worries, gorgeous."

"I'm on the pill."

My hands still as I undid my belt, looked to her.

"That mean I can take you bare? Do I have permission to come deep inside that pussy?"

I hadn't known she could flush a prettier shade of pink, but she did.

"Yes."

Fuck, yes. With increased urgency, I opened my jeans, reached in, and pulled out my dick. Gripped the base and stroked it from root to tip, all while she watched with widening eyes.

"Gotta make sure you're nice and ready for this."

6

SUMMER

OH MY GOD. *Oh my God.*

Boone was definitely proportioned. His dick was impressive. My pussy clenched and dripped with need when I should perhaps be afraid of whether that thing was going to fit or split me in two.

I'd only ever had sex with Marty. He was just shy of six feet tall and was slender. His cock had been–now I definitely knew–small. Compared to Boone, it had been like being fucked with a little pinky finger.

Boone was going to fuck me like I needed *with that?* It was like a baseball bat. Soda can. Anything big one could imagine to describe it.

Thankfully, I was very, very wet and very, very

eager. Curious, too, to discover what I'd been missing. And get it.

He stroked himself one more time then moved to my other sock, tossing it, too, aside.

My jeans and panties were gone before I could even blink and–

"Oh!" I cried as he dropped to his knees once again, this time onto the soft carpet at the side of my bed. He didn't waste time while flinging my legs over his shoulders and put his mouth on me.

There.

"Boone!" I cried, arching my back. I tried to push away with my heels, and he instantly lifted his head.

I couldn't believe I was going to have a conversation with the man with his head *between my thighs.* That dark hair, that beard, the glistening mouth, the *need* I saw in his gaze.

"Permission to eat you out," he growled.

Those words made me wetter, and he took a deep breath, his nostrils flaring. He was patient, waiting for my answer.

"Yes, but I've never–" I bit my lip, not wanting to admit that Marty had never, not once, gone down on me. Said he didn't like it, that he didn't like the taste of pussy. I also didn't want to admit that he'd never once given me an orgasm. I'd only ever given those to myself in the shower when I was alone.

Boone's eyes narrowed. "You have now."

Because I said yes, he went to work and with a renewed sense of purpose, as if he was going to make this the first–and best–experience ever. He licked me from–*holy shit*–my asshole all the way to my clit.

I jerked off the bed at the feelings his tongue brought about. One huge hand settled across my stomach and held me in place.

Then he went to work. By work, I meant he licked my clit and slid a thick finger inside me. Then out. Then in. Then–

I had no idea what he was doing down there, but he got me to come with a pace he should be proud of. One second, I was clawing at his hair and arching my back, the next I screamed his name and clenched around his finger in the most powerful and intense orgasm of my life.

I panted and tried to catch my breath, but wow. I'd never come that hard before or come with something in me.

I wasn't going to dwell on how shitty things must've been with Marty if *this* was what it was really like, and Boone hadn't even gotten inside me yet. He was still dressed, even!

I was sated and relaxed and felt so amazing that I was hooked.

"Another," he said.

I lifted my head. "Another?"

His beard was coated with my arousal. His cheeks flushed, jaw clenched tight. He was into this.

"Another finger," he clarified. "Another orgasm."

When he pulled back, then slid two fingers into me and curled them to rub over some place inside me that was magical and life changing, my head flopped back, and I let go.

7

BOONE

HONEY. Fuck me. She tasted like sticky, sweet honey. And she dripped for me. It was in my beard, all over my hand. On my tongue.

Soon, it was going to coat my dick, too. But my pleasure was secondary to pleasuring my mate. Learning what satisfied her.

She'd started to say no man had ever eaten her pussy before? That made me want to go find that soon-to-be ex of hers and teach him a lesson or two about how to treat a woman.

That began on your knees. Worshipping her body. Knowing she was aroused and needy, sated, and ready for your dick. Then, only then, should a guy even consider himself.

Only when she'd come again did I push up to rid her of her t-shirt and bra. She'd been sweaty and sated and laid all bare and perfect as I stripped down.

Pulling her up the bed so her head rested on the pillow, I loomed over her, nudging her knees apart and settling between her parted thighs.

Even with two orgasms and being stretched on my fingers, her pussy was going to be so fucking tight. I lined up at her slick entrance, met her eyes. Slowly sank into her.

"Fuck, Summer. So perfect."

Fuck. *Fuck.* She felt so good. Hot, wet. Her walls rippled around the head. I hadn't gotten in farther than that.

"Good girl. Take me, and I'll give you what you need."

Bending her knee, she brought her leg up, so it was along my side, I sank deeper.

Oh shit, I wasn't going to make it. I was going to come from playing Just The Tip.

"Boone," she breathed, her hands going to my arms, sliding up and down my sides, feeling me.

She was so small beneath me, I couldn't kiss her and fuck her this way without snapping my back.

I rolled us so she was on top, and that move had her dropping all the way onto me.

"BOONE!" she cried again, her inner walls rippling and clenching down around me trying to adjust.

I set my hand on her stomach, felt the head of my dick inside her. Jackknifing up, I kissed her, bent my knees, so she sat in the crook of my body. Protected and impaled.

With my hands on her hips, I lifted and lowered, helped her fuck herself on me as we kissed. Her knees barely touched the bed at my sides.

She quickly gave over to the pleasure, her eyes slipping closed, head tipping back. Her hair wasn't long, but it tickled my bare thighs.

This was good. Perfect. I'd never felt anything like the tight, wet fist of her pussy. My wolf was thrilled we had our mate right where we wanted her. Already satisfied and craving more. Bare and ready for my mark.

But it wasn't enough, so I rolled us again, reached between us, and rubbed her clit, getting her off once more.

As she cried out my name, I fucked the hell out of her, the headboard slamming against the wall.

"Mine. Mine. Fuck, gorgeous," I growled. Sweat dripped from my brow. My hand clenched in the sheets and tore the cotton.

Another deep thrust, and there was a crack, the bed breaking and tipping on one side. I didn't stop–I couldn't–my wolf was right at the surface, dying to claim her.

She'd given me permission to fuck her bare, to fill her with my cum.

It took all my effort not to mark her as I shoved into her pussy so fucking deep and came, filling her over and over, slamming my jaws closed to hide my extended fangs.

Summer gasped and moaned in pleasure, arching to receive me. Her tight channel pulsed and contracted around me. Her eyes were closed, blonde hair splayed in a light halo around her.

My wolf was pissed I hadn't marked her, but the rest of me reveled in the fucking glory of coming in her. Of pleasing my mate. Of having her under me. Of breathing in her scent mixed with the smell of her arousal and my cum.

I gave a low rumble of approval. My dick was still hard. It wasn't going down anytime soon.

Her eyes flew open and widened, then she smiled.

I blinked rapidly, realizing my wolf's eyes were probably showing.

She drew in a breath. "You're one of them, aren't you?"

8

———

SUMMER

SHOCK STRUCK BOONE'S EXPRESSION, and he went perfectly still.

His eyes *had* changed color as I'd thought. I'd have sworn they were brown a moment ago, the same shade as his beard, but right now, as he loomed sated and large over me, they glowed a pale shade of green. Cash green. And when I said they glowed, they had the same glint that a cat's or dog's had in the darkness. Like they were able to see in the dark when you couldn't.

Slowly, Boone eased out of me, sat back on his heels. Wow, he was still huge and hard, now coated in my arousal. A bead of cum seeped still from the little slit at the top.

He did that thing he'd done when he sat at the end of the bar, holding very still, like he didn't want to spook me. His eyes held mine.

"What do you mean, baby?" he asked, his voice low.

I suddenly wished I had said nothing. I didn't want him to lie to me about what he was like Natalie had. That had hurt my feelings when she'd done it. Rand was a werewolf. I knew because I'd seen him during the full moon. I'd looked out the window of my over-the-garage apartment to see a huge wolf run up to their back door then transform into a butt-naked man and walk right in the house. Not any butt-naked man—Rand. I'd never seen him naked before, or since, but I recognized him.

That had been one hell of a surprise.

I wasn't supposed to know what he was, obviously. In fact, Natalie had lied right to my face when I asked about it the next morning, so I didn't press the issue. It had been that important of a secret that my dear friend, the one who was generous enough to put me up in her extra space, felt she couldn't tell me the truth. After that butt-baring incident, I looked for clues that Rand was a werewolf.

There were a lot when the secret was known.

For one thing, the ranch that abutted this one was called Wolf Ranch. The brothers who owned it—Rob,

Colton, and Boyd–had the last name Wolf. Every full moon, at least the few I'd been here, Natalie went up to Wolf Ranch to hang out in the big house with the ladies. I also heard the howling of wolves up on the mountain. Not only did Rand run alone when it wasn't a full moon, but it seemed he ran with *others*. There were lots of shifters around here.

Then there was the eye color thing. I'd seen Rand's change when he was getting hot for Natalie, especially if it was close to the full moon. It was one thing to see them flirt or a little extra PDA in the kitchen, him cupping her ass or whispering something that made her blush, but the eyes... no human could do what Rand's did. Then I realized Cody's eyes did the same thing when his wife came around the bar. It was as if they couldn't control themselves, that their need for their women was so potent that they *changed*.

Now, Boone's were doing the same thing. For me.

I also couldn't miss how Cody and Rand were hella strong. So was Boone–I'd watched him pick up that huge trash barrel full of glass bottles at the bar like it held feathers–and he was even bigger than either of his friends.

As far as I could tell, these shifters weren't danger-ous. Rand and Cody were both nice as could be. I didn't hear about dead bodies being found after the full moon or anytime in Cooper Valley although that was taking things to the extreme in my head. They weren't vampires or serial killers. They were shifters.

Natalie didn't seem scared for me, and she didn't seem afraid of her husband or any of the others from Wolf Ranch who I'd met. I knew she wouldn't have invited me to move out here to stay with her until I got back on my feet if it wasn't safe. In fact, she'd promised Rand would protect me if Marty showed up and tried to drag me back to LA.

I reached out and stroked Boone's thick beard. It was so soft... and had been between my thighs just as I'd imagined.

"Are you a werewolf?" My voice sounded hoarse.

He nuzzled the hollow in the front of my shoulder, dropping a kiss there. "What do you know about were-wolves?" His voice was deep and husky.

Ugh. He didn't answer my question. I really didn't want him to gaslight me about this.

Marty gaslit me every day of our marriage, telling me something like my outfit was too slutty, then when I got upset about it, he pounced on that. Like it was my fault he was getting angry about wearing something that wasn't remotely inappropriate.

I couldn't take mind games like that from a man again. I'd rather never be in a relationship than have a man who belittled me that way a second longer. It'd taken me years to recognize what he'd been doing, how easily I fell for it all, lost my family, my friends. My confidence.

It was back now, and I wasn't giving it away again. Ever.

I met his gaze with a hint of defiance. "I know Natalie lied to me when I asked her if Rand was one."

Rather than shut down, his expression softened and opened. His lips quirked a little at the edges. He lowered his head and... oh my, flicked his tongue over my erect nipple. "That's because you weren't supposed to know, baby. It's a secret. But it's okay now. You're mine."

His?

I stiffened at that, even though my body seemed to enjoy his assertion, my pussy clenching in an aftershock. It was too possessive. Too... all consuming.

"I'm not yours," I said immediately and decisively.

His expression clouded, and he settled along my side, leaning on one elbow to prop his head with his hand and tracing my nipple with the index finger of his other hand. Lazily. Slowly. As if he didn't have a care in the world. As if I hadn't just asked him if he was a werewolf. As if *he* hadn't raised a huge red flag with the use of one word: mine.

I looked at his thick finger as it moved over my skin with fascination. It was so large. As large as a normal man's dick. I knew what it felt like to have that digit inside me. In fact, I knew what it was like to have two of them inside me.

"I know your divorce isn't complete yet," he said with a slight shrug of his broad shoulder. "Cody told me. I don't care about human laws."

Human laws. Wow.

A little thrill zinged through my body. It was confirmed. He wasn't human. This giant, burly man was something extra. Something stronger. More animalistic. Far more dangerous than a normal man. Far more dangerous than Marty, possibly. And I was in bed with him. A bed that had broken because he'd been so... vigorous. My pussy was sore, but he hadn't hurt me.

Still, I should be scared after what I'd been through with my soon-to-be-ex husband. Part of me was suddenly a bit nervous, but surprisingly, mostly I was turned on.

Excited.

Happy he trusted me enough to admit it. He hadn't hidden what he was. He hadn't tried to skirt around the topic or switch topics entirely. He hadn't tried to distract me with another orgasm, but his playing with my nipple was certainly turning me on again.

"What is it I'm not supposed to know?" Again, I put a little challenge in my voice. I dared him to tell me because he hadn't actually said the words.

His lips twitched again, and I remembered how they felt pressed against mine. Lower, too.

"We're not werewolves–at least we don't call ourselves that," he explained. "Werewolves are the monsters of folklore. We're just another species–wolf shifters."

My heart beat a little faster at his explanation. *We.* He was admitting that it wasn't just him. There was a whole pack of them, like I suspected.

"Don't be sore at Natalie," he added. "There are strict pack rules about not letting humans in on our secret." So Natalie wasn't a shifter. She hadn't kept *that* huge secret from me the entire time we'd been friends. No doubt she learned about them when she moved here to Cooper Valley, too.

Boone molded his large, calloused hand around my breast and squeezed. "How did you figure it out?"

I arched my back, pressing my small breast into his palm. Okay, I was a little distracted. "I saw Rand as a wolf and then shift out of it on the full moon."

His hand stroked down my side, sliding over the curve of my hip then tucking beneath my ass to squeeze. His gaze lifted to meet mine. Gone was the green hue. "You're not scared?"

I held his now-brown eyes. "Should I be? Of you? Of any wolf shifter?"

He shook his head. "No, baby. No wolf will ever

hurt you. Especially not me." He trailed kisses along the ribs beneath my breast and up around the side. God, his gentleness was a turn on because I didn't expect it of him. Someone who'd just broken my bed was brushing my skin with feather light touches.

"Thank you for not lying about it," I said quietly.

It felt like relief. Like I was now in the inner circle that I'd been barred from before. Maybe it was just all my middle school issues coming to the surface, but I'd hated being left out. No one liked to feel like everyone knew a secret but you.

"Ask me anything, baby," he said. "I want to explain it all to you."

Really? "No secrets?"

No making me feel crazy for asking in the first place?

Nope. He *wanted* me to know.

"No secrets," he confirmed.

"So you transform during the full moon? Are you... um, compelled to? Are you dangerous when you're in wolf form?"

Boone's eyes crinkled like he found me cute. "We can shift anytime, but the urge is stronger with the full moon. It's not a compulsion to do it if a shifter has control of his wolf. It can be a problem for teen wolves or a shifter who's on edge from anger or lust. Kind of like my dick getting hard. I can get hard watching a sex scene in a movie or waking up in the morning. Both I can control, but around you? My dick's gonna always be hard. *That* will be hard to control." He rolled his hip, and I felt the big, hard truth behind those words.

At the word *lust*, his eyes turned green again.

Was the moon close to full tonight?

I glanced out the window. No. A half-moon.

"Is that why you grabbed me tonight?" I ventured, my insecurity sinking in again thinking maybe he'd chosen me to... scratch an itch that was unavoidable on or near a full moon, like that morning wood.

His gaze caressed my face as if he was trying to memorize it. Every inch of me. "Yes. I caught your scent in that crowd, and I instantly knew you were mine."

There it was again–that assertion. *Mine.*

It was starting to make me itchy. To feel a little worried, like I'd made a dumb choice and put myself in a bad situation.

"I'm sorry if I scared you," he told me. "Grabbed you like that. I just lost control for a moment until I realized you weren't a she-wolf and had no idea what I was about. Sometimes I don't know my own strength. Sometimes–never mind."

Logically, I knew what he said shouldn't give me offense, but years of being belittled by Marty made me feel suddenly inadequate.

I wasn't a she-wolf. I didn't know what was going on.

He probably wanted a she-wolf. Wanted someone who would understand him. Who wouldn't mind being grabbed and manhandled by a giant. What guy would want my kind of insecurities?

"Awkward, right?" I played it off, trying to roll away and get off the bed.

"Hold up." Boone looped that tree-trunk-sized arm around my waist and pulled me back against him, just like he had in the bar. Now, though, we were naked. Now, we were alone.

I stiffened. Some alarms were starting to go off.

First–that thing he kept saying about me belonging to him.

That was wrong. Dead wrong.

Marty treated me like a possession he could control, and was this what Boone wanted, too?

I didn't care how talented his dick was, I wasn't going back there, not ever.

Second, I was feeling bruised over the she-wolf comment, like it was impossible for me to ever measure up to what he really wanted. I could color my hair, let it grow out, wear colored contacts, but I sure as hell couldn't turn into a wolf.

And third, if I tried to get away from Boone's hold right now, I couldn't. He was that big and strong. It would be physically impossible. I wasn't fit enough, and I knew how powerful he was. It wasn't just words I had to protect myself from but, now, something physical, too.

I'd been manhandled by a jealous, possessive husband for such a long time, so anything that smelled anything like possession freaked me out.

"What just happened, Summer?" Boone's voice was a deep rumble. He held me captive, but it felt more like a hug from behind.

Part of me loved it because a *normal,* not broken woman would crave a man/shifter like Boone to hold her.

Another part was freaking out–the part that kept me safe these days.

"Did I offend you, baby?" he wondered. "What did I say? Shit, I'm an idiot."

No, I was an idiot. Of course, he hadn't meant to hurt my feelings.

"Let me go," I murmured, testing.

How long would this behemoth of a guy follow my rules? Was it over now that he got laid?

The muscles in his arm went slack although he didn't move it away from me. "I don't want to." I heard regret in his voice. "Not ever."

"You're... you're freaking me out," I admitted.

He instantly released me and sat up on the bed,

probably feeling my words tremble right along with my body. "Shit. I'm sorry, Summer."

I rolled off the now-lopsided bed and tried to change the subject. Eyed the damage. "You broke the bed."

"*We.* We broke the bed." He grinned. "I'll make a new one. A sturdier one."

He'd make a bed? Seriously. "Are you a woodworker?"

He nodded. "My brother Roy's the real wood-worker. I'm a lumberjack, mostly. I chop down trees. Have my own business. My other brother, Ace, has a Christmas tree farm up on the mountain. Don't worry, we'll make something sturdier and replace it."

Lumberjack. Of course, he was a lumberjack. He looked like one. Acted like one from the way he seemed to be almost... feral, happier in nature than around people. But there was something about him, an awareness that indicated he was far sharper than a simple mountain man. He was quiet. Observed. Studied. Saved his words for when it was important to speak.

He eyed me as I stood away from him, my arms going around my waist. His cum started to slip down my thighs, a reminder of what we'd done. That might be washed away in the shower, but I'd feel him, my pussy sore, for days.

"Who hurt you, Summer?"

The question took my breath away. I swayed on my feet, dizzy from standing up too fast. Or maybe from the bluntness of the question. How it hit so close to why I was freaking out.

Boone got up, too. Slowly. Carefully. He stalked toward me. "Who?" he repeated.

I swallowed hard, licked my lips. "My husband. I'm not a cheater, us being together. He is. We're... separated, and as soon as he signs the papers... if he does, then, then I'll be single." The words came out in a big rush.

His fists clenched once then opened. Relaxed. "I know, baby. I didn't think anything like that about you. Not once." He cocked his head, reached out, and gently took one of my hands.

His eyebrow winged up. "He the one who hurt you?"

Tears rushed to my eyes, and he knew the answer without me saying anything.

They weren't over what happened with Marty. That was over. I left and would never go back. But I burned with the shame of it. Of what being with him for so long turned me into. I didn't want to be that person ever again. I didn't want Boone to see me as that person. I didn't identify as a woman who would put herself in a domestic abuse situation.

But I was. He saw it.

I wanted to be the spunky young country singer who won best song at the state fair six years ago. The one who still had her whole life ahead of her. Not a washed-up, married to a controlling cop who got violent at the end version of that young woman. Not the fool who let her husband convince her to quit her job pursuing her music full-time without realizing he was picking off her resources one by one. Isolating her from her friends. Making her weak and dependent, so it was harder to leave.

But I was.

Boone, as if trying to keep from scaring a skittish horse, reached out slowly, oh so slowly, and wrapped me up in his arms. "Easy," he whispered. "That's it. My good girl."

This time, when I felt comfort in his hold instead of fear, I didn't mind. I loved the fierce bear hug that lifted me right off the ground.

"I'll kill him," Boone growled, switching from gentle to fierce. Not at me, but for me. "Give me his name."

9

BOONE

My wolf snarled, ready to eviscerate her ex. I needed to kill him. Summer was scared of me. Me! After what we'd done, how she'd trusted me with her body so beautifully and now was retreating, these ingrained fears that were brought about by another? It was blatantly obvious someone had hurt her.

Sure, I was big as fuck, but I'd learned long ago that I had to be careful. That my size could be used as a weapon. My father had wanted me to challenge Rob Wolf for alpha after his parents were killed in that horrible car crash. He and I fought about it for over a month. With words and then fists and then a full-on fight. I'd won, but the cost was a ruined family. I'd disobeyed and then almost killed my father.

Because of that aggression, that level of destruction, I fled the mountain and headed to college, the only option I knew at the time. I'd been sixteen, too smart to stay in high school. Too smart not to get a full ride to several Ivy League colleges.

I'd planned to turn them down, stay in Cooper Valley, and start a business with my brothers. Instead, I'd packed my bags and left for the East Coast. The further I was from the pack, the safer they'd all be from a monster like me who beat up his own father.

I knew my strength, and now I knew when to use it. For Summer, it'd be to finish her ex.

Nobody hurt my mate and lived to tell about it. I didn't know the extent of what he'd done, but it was enough that she was afraid of me because of him. She had my cum dripping down her thighs. I saw it. I scented it. Yet, she still trembled and not from the orgasms.

"*No.*" There was a firmness in Summer's voice, and she tried to push away from me.

I cursed inwardly. She'd made me promise to honor her *no*. A rule that was going to be a hard oath to keep because I wanted blood.

So did my wolf. It was our job to protect her and removing him from this earth should give her the peace of mind to move on, that no one would touch her or spew shit to make her feel anything less than perfect.

She didn't know shifter justice.

I reluctantly freed her, scrubbing a hand across my beard, licked my lips, and got her sweet taste. "No, you won't give me his name, or no, I can't kill him?" I looked for wiggle room in the rule.

Her brows knitted together in confusion, probably because no one had ever said they'd finish someone for her. "No. To both."

Fuck. Well, I was definitely going to look into the guy and memorize his face, so I'd recognize him if he ever showed up in Cooper Valley. She'd only said I couldn't kill the fucker. That didn't mean I wouldn't keep him the hell away from her.

The town sheriff, Levi, was also a shifter wolf. His job dealt in human law, but he also followed pack and shifter justice. If I couldn't kill her ex, then I could enlist his help.

But, I was being a dick. Caring for my mate now trumped any need for revenge. Barely. I held up my hands but waited for her tentative gaze to meet mine. "Okay. You make the rules, baby. I follow them. You're safe with me. I'll keep saying it until you believe it."

To release my pent-up aggression, I picked up the bed and tore the three remaining legs off it, so it would be level for the night. It rested six inches lower now, but we weren't going to roll onto the floor.

Summer stared at me with wide eyes. I'd done that with an ease as if I'd removed twigs.

Well, fuck. That probably didn't help her feel any safer with me.

I looked from the bed to her. "Wanna go up to my place?" I offered, a little sheepish. "Up on the mountain?"

She gave a tiny shake of her head.

I gestured toward the bed. "Sorry, did that freak you out, too?"

She rubbed her lips together. "Um...a little. Yeah. You're strong."

"Damn." I rubbed my forehead. "I'm so bad at this." How the hell did I get her back in that bed with my arms around her? "Permission to pick you up and carry you back to that bed, so I can lick your pussy again?"

A small smile tugged at the corners of her mouth, and the tension in her shoulders relaxed. "You really like to do that, huh?"

"Fuck yes, and I'm happy to prove it." I grinned, and she couldn't miss how my dick got harder.

"Okay." Her voice was soft, but her cheeks were flushed. Yeah, she'd liked what we'd done and wanted more.

I'd spend the rest of my night with my head between her thighs if it made her happy.

In an instant, I was on her, picking her up to straddle my waist. Her honey scent curled in my nostrils, soothing my riled wolf. I felt our combined fluids that coated her pussy and thighs smear across my abs.

Mark her, my wolf insisted.

Not tonight. I held him back as I carried her back to the now-lowered bed and carefully laid her in the center.

I rolled her to her side and arranged my larger body around hers, protectively. "You're safe, Summer," I murmured in her ear then nipped the shell of it.

Her scent made me dizzy with desire, but I kept my wolf leashed.

Laying kisses along the column of her neck, I said, "I'm gonna want to kill anyone who hurts you, but you will always be safe with me. And I will always respect your no. Okay?"

I thought I caught the scent of her tears, and it slashed a hole right through the middle of my chest.

"Okay," she whispered.

I closed my eyes and willed my wolf to quiet. My mate was in my arms. She wasn't ready for me to mark her, but she wanted her pussy licked. She was so easy to lift up and set over my head, her knees by my ears.

"Boone?"

She looked down at me a little confused.

I grinned, breathed in her honey scent right from the source. "You said okay to me licking your pussy. You're gonna sit on my face and let me do it."

Her eyes widened, and she squirmed, then nodded.

"That's my good girl."

I hooked her thighs and pulled her down onto my mouth. Got to work. This was my job now, satisfying my woman. The sound of her pleasured screams echoed in my ears as I made her come again and again, until she wasn't the least bit scared of me. That she knew all I'd ever give her was pleasure.

Tomorrow, I'd get her to quit her job at Cody's and come live with me on the mountain. Tomorrow, I'd explain what it meant to be my mate.

10

SUMMER

THE NEXT MORNING, we were in Rand and Natalie's kitchen. While I had my own little kitchenette in my apartment, my routine was to have coffee with them in the morning.

It'd been two years since they got together and had spent most of that time rebuilding the farmhouse and getting it just the way they wanted it. From what Natalie had told me, she'd inherited the entire ranch from an uncle who hadn't made any updates since the 1970s. She'd met Rand when she hired him to make overhauls, but then the entire place was burned down in an accidental fire, and Rand had to rebuild from scratch. With the rebuild, they stayed with the old farmhouse feel, but it had modern appliances, gleaming white counters, and glossy wood floors. The cabinets were a mix of white and gray, to accentuate the farmhouse core.

They also had a very modern, very elaborate coffeemaker. I was at the banquette that looked out over the snowy backyard and the mountains beyond, sipping my mocha. It even had steamed milk. Natalie sat at the kitchen table, and the guys–Rand and Boone–leaned against the counter.

"I'm sorry I didn't tell you." Natalie reached across the wooden table and took my hand when I sat down. "It wasn't my place to tell, and I was protecting not just Rand but the entire pack." She'd pulled her red curls back into a ponytail, and her brown eyes were warm but showed she was worried that I hated her.

I smiled, my other hand wrapped around my mug. I was in soft leggings, thick socks, and a sweater with a wide turtleneck collar. It had snowed while Boone and I slept, a few inches that made everything outside gleam. "I understand. I would guess some would think you're crazy and have you committed for saying shifter wolves existed, and some would blab it to the world."

"You won't." She glanced at Boone and gave him a sly smile. "Not now that you found your mate. I'm so happy for you."

I frowned. "Mate?"

Rand pushed off the counter and gave Boone a steely look. His dark hair was still wet from the shower, making his blue eyes pop. "Um, she doesn't know?"

I was starting to feel unsure all over again. Doesn't know what?

"She knows," Boone told Rand.

Rand cocked his head. "You sure?"

"Guys," Natalie called then pointed to me. "*She's* right here. Why don't you ask her?"

"Um, yeah, I'm right here," I repeated, meaning Natalie, too, seemed to be talking about me as if I wasn't here.

"You're my mate," Boone said casually then took a sip of his coffee.

I looked between the three of them. "Um, what?"

"He's your mate, honey," Natalie said, her voice soft. Her face was lit with satisfaction, which meant it was a good thing?

Natalie looked to Rand with nothing but love in her eyes. "Rand's my mate."

"Meaning," I said, drawing out the word. "He's your husband?"

"He is that, but marriage, that's a human thing. On paper, legally, we're married. But he's a shifter, and they don't care about those things."

"I cared that you cared, Red," Rand said gently.

"But Nat's right. Shifters don't need a marriage license to be together."

"Because I got your scent, and my wolf immediately knew you belonged to me," Boone stated.

I stiffened. A door slammed shut in my chest. I set my mug down with a thunk and shook my head. "No. I won't *belong* to anyone ever again. I did that once, and... and I lost myself."

Natalie grabbed my hand again and squeezed. "I know, but this is different. Boone, in his growly way, is saying that a shifter scents his mate, even if she's a human, and that's good enough for them. They know you're the one. No marriage license or wedding needed."

"So that's why you kept saying 'mine' last night?"

Natalie's lips quirked.

"You didn't seem to mind it when you were sitting–"

I held up my hand, and I felt my cheeks flush hot. Was he actually going to tell our friends over coffee that I'd sat on his face and held onto the broken headboard as he made me come?

Yes, it seemed he was.

"You are mine. We'll get your things together, leave here, and head up the mountain to my cabin."

I slid back on the bench seat. "Um. What? Get my things?"

Boone nodded. He had on the clothes from the night before. His hair was a little messed up from my fingers and sleep, but he still looked good.

He nodded. "Yes, we will have you packed up in no time."

"You want me to *move in with you?*" I screeched.

Oh no. Huh-uh. This wasn't happening. I wasn't even divorced yet. It took me three years to figure out how to get away from Marty. There was no way I was putting myself in that situation ever again.

"You're my mate. You belong with me."

"Up a mountain?" I thought Natalie's ranch was remote, a few miles outside of a small town, but in the woods? "My car can't make it up there, not with the snow."

He shook his head. "I will drive you. You don't need your car."

This was why people didn't have one-night stands with strangers. What looked hot and sexy at night was not the same with the harsh morning light. Boone was possessive. He was expecting me to move up a freaking mountain to live with him. To give up my cozy little apartment here for him. To a place where I wouldn't be able to drive my car and have him take me around.

I held up my hand. "No. No. This isn't happening."

Rand set his hand on Boone's arm. "Gotta chill, man. You're scaring her."

Boone's eyes widened. Clearly, he didn't even know what he'd been saying was bat-shit crazy and threw up more red flags than someone in the Navy doing semaphore.

"How is being my mate scary?" Boone asked, looking completely confused. "Baby, I told you I'd never hurt you. You belong with me, and I'll take care of you. I have more money than I'll need in several life-times. You don't even have to work at Cody's any longer."

Natalie rolled her eyes and groaned.

I slid along the bench and popped to my feet, my coffee abandoned.

"No," I said flatly, holding my hand out. "I don't want that. I don't want to quit my job and live isolated on a mountain where you control my every move."

"Of course, he doesn't mean it like it sounds," Natalie said, playing Switzerland. "He's going to finish his coffee, give you a kiss goodbye, and–"

"What?" Boone asked, cutting Natalie off.

But she pushed on.

"–see you tonight at Cody's for karaoke. I've been wanting to hear you sing again ever since you moved here."

"But–"

"Let's go plow the driveway." Rand grabbed Boone's biceps and tried to tug him toward the back door.

I looked at my feet, afraid I'd give in to whatever Boone said next at the look in his eye.

"Summer, you're mine," he said. "My mate. Don't be afraid."

"Come on, big guy," Rand said. With the back door open, cold air ripped through the room.

Boone didn't say anything else but left with Rand.

When the door shut behind them, Natalie said, "Men. They're idiots. If they weren't good with their dicks, would we even need them?"

I turned and looked at her then burst into laughter.

She laughed, too.

11

———

BOONE

We trudged through the fresh snow toward the furthest garage bay. Rand typed in a code on the keypad, and the door slid up.

"You know she has an asshole for an ex?" Rand asked.

Our breaths came out in frosty clouds. I was big enough where I didn't feel the sharp bite of cold, but my eyes didn't like the bright glint of sun on the snow, so I squinted.

"Yeah. Cody told me she was married, getting a divorce. And I think he hurt her," I said, remembering what she'd shared the night before. The lack of pussy eating, too.

"Yeah, he was controlling. Like dangerous control-ling. Told her what to wear. Took away her job. Her friends. Isolated her."

My eyes widened as I followed him into the garage and to the pickup truck that had a plow on the front. He climbed into the driver's seat, and I climbed in on the other side. He started up the engine, drove out of the garage, then lowered the plow and started clearing the snow.

"She's only now realizing how fucked up it all was. Now that she's safe."

"Shit, I don't want to do that," I said.

He glanced at me for a second. "I know, but you told her, a human, a human who had a dickhead controlling ex, that she was yours, that she belonged to you, that you were moving her up to a remote cabin in the mountains where she couldn't take her car, and she'd quit her job because she was your mate. Oh, and you two met less than twelve hours ago."

Fuuuuuuck.

I saw his point. "Being human makes it hard for her to understand."

He huffed as he steered around a curve in his drive halfway to the road.

"Trust me, I know how hard it is to get a human female to understand what's in our nature. You should feel lucky that she knows what you are. Nat saw me shift as a kid, so she knew, too, but the others... they had a fucking hard time trying to explain what the hell was going on."

The air in the truck was just starting to warm up, but I barely noticed.

"That does sound harder. I couldn't imagine getting Summer to believe what I am if she can't understand that 'mine' doesn't mean I want to possess her."

"But you do," Rand countered. "Nat is mine. My possession. My *obsession.* The important thing is for her to know that it's putting her on a pedestal. Making her the most important thing in your life. That you'd do anything for her."

"I would," I vowed, nodding.

He pushed the snow directly across the dirt road and to the berm on the far side, then did a three-point turn to head back down his drive again, plowing the other side.

"Including giving her room," Rand added. "Leaving here without her and seeing her tonight at Cody's."

I clenched my fists on my thighs. "Why the hell do I have to do that?"

"She needs to lead her own life," he explained.

I frowned. "But I have to keep her safe."

Rand sighed. "I'm watching out for her. Cody does at work. She's safe. If her ex shows up–"

I turned my head, looked at my friend and fellow

packmate. "If her ex shows up, he's a dead man. Levi might be sheriff, but we will mete out pack justice."

Rand clenched his jaw. "Agreed."

"Look, I know you're smart as fuck. That investment you told me about has quadrupled in value. But a mate is a different thing entirely. There is no textbook about it. There's no logic. You can't use your brain here. You have to use your heart... and maybe your dick. For once, let her lead."

12

SUMMER

"I'M SCARED OF HIM, NAT," I said. I'd returned to the table and picked my coffee back up. It would be a shame to waste such delicious caffeine.

She cocked her head. "Honey, I can tell you until I'm blue in the face that Boone would never hurt you. Ever. If he scented you, then you are his mate, and it's in his very biology to do anything and everything to make you safe and happy."

"Like Rand does with you?" I'd seen how he treated her, and I was envious. It was the first thing that made me realize how truly awful Marty was. Would Boone be like that with me?

She nodded. "Yes, like Rand does with me. I will

admit, at first, he was kind of... smothering. When they go all in for their mate, they go *all* in."

That sure sounded familiar. "Were you scared?"

She gave me a soft smile. "No. Freaked, maybe, but Rand has only been sweet. Growly, for sure, but kind. I feel safe with him and all the guys in the pack."

"He... Boone, he doesn't seem to know what to say. Like everything that comes out of his mouth sets me off."

"Boone's an interesting one. Did you know he went to college in New York? Got an MBA. He lived and worked there for years."

My eyes widened. I didn't think he was dumb, but he seemed... hyperfocused on me.

"Shifters live in big cities like that?" I wondered.

Natalie shrugged. "Maybe some, but they are pack animals, and they love to run on full moons. Pretty hard to do in a huge city like that."

I frowned, studied the pretty glazing on my mug Natalie told me once had been made by her friend Joy. "Then why'd he go there?"

She took a sip of her coffee. "This was way before my time, but Rand told me that when the last alpha died, Boone was a possibility to replace him because he was his–the alpha's–nephew. Rob Wolf and Boone are first cousins. Boone's father, the old alpha's brother-in-law, wanted Boone to challenge Rob for the position. They argued. Boone and his dad, I mean. Fought even. His dad was hurt from the confrontation, and Boone left for Columbia University."

Wow, that didn't sound like the Boone I knew. "How old was he?"

She took a sip of coffee. "Sixteen, I think. Boone and Rob are around the same age."

My eyes widened. "Sixteen and he went to college?"

She nodded and smiled. "Yeah. He's *that* smart. Got a fancy Wall Street job that dealt with rich people's money. Can you see him in a suit?"

I couldn't. Surely, they'd have been custom made. No matter how appealing he'd have looked, I liked him in flannel. Or naked. "Then why'd he come back?"

Natalie shrugged. "Not sure. Something bad must've happened because he's pretty much isolated himself on the mountain ever since. Which, circling back to you, is why he's acting all weird. He's never had a mate before."

"Like, no ex-mates?"

She shook her head. "You only get one. Some might settle for a relationship with another shifter if they give up on finding their mate, but no. He's never been like this with anyone else. You've got to give him a little slack. He might seem so big and strong and brave, but he's got his own baggage. I think a lot of it."

I frowned, suddenly seeing Boone as more than

just a huge guy. He was strong but had worries and feelings and concerns like everyone else.

"I don't blame you for being scared, especially after what Marty did, but that was Marty. You can't put his behavior on every guy you meet. Especially on Boone because his growly nature isn't going to change. You just need to take some time to start trusting him."

I bit my lip. "We, um... had sex."

She smiled. "I figured if he came down for coffee with you. And?" She waggled her brows.

"And it was amazing." I grinned back, blushing at remembering how hot it had been. I never imagined it could ever be like that. What I'd had with Marty, my own husband, for years, paled in comparison to one night with Boone. "So, yeah, I trusted him enough to bring him home."

"It's a start," she replied. "A good start. Just give him a chance. But, I do like how you're putting your foot down. Don't let any guy, shifter or not, walk all over you."

I huffed. "I know that. Now."

"Good. Got an outfit for karaoke tonight?" she asked, switching topics.

Cody's had karaoke once a month. Natalie knew I loved to sing and had put my name down with Cody weeks ago to be on the list to perform. She'd even told the other girls, Audrey, her sister Marina, and the others whose men were part of Wolf Ranch, to come and watch. Maybe participate, too. It was the first time I'd be singing anywhere outside of my shower since I moved here.

Not since the last time I'd performed when Marty made an ugly scene over the guys whistling for me while I was on stage in a mini-skirt. He'd hauled me out of there and berated me the entire way home. Told me I couldn't perform in public anymore, even though he'd been the one who offered to support me to get my music career off the ground.

"Um, I don't think I have to wear anything special for karaoke," I countered, thinking maybe jeans and a thick turtleneck sweater.

Her eyes widened. "Not for karaoke but your big night? Definitely." She tipped her chin. "The guys are plowing the drive. When it's all clear, we'll go shopping in town and find you something to make you feel like the music star I know you are. Plus, we want to knock Boone's socks off, right?"

I couldn't help the grin. "Yes. To both."

She clapped her hands.

"Oh, I can't wait to see his face when he hears you sing. That man's gonna fall like a tree in the woods. Hard and fast. Honey, I hope you have lots of panties because he's gonna rip through them all."

Heat flooded my body. Oh my. And, yes, please.

13

BOONE

I PULLED up and parked my truck at Cody's after the longest fucking day of my life.

Being away from my unmarked mate drove my wolf insane. Because of that, I'd needed to shift and run so badly that I'd driven back up the mountain and let my wolf out.

Even that hadn't done much to relieve the pressure inside me, so I'd taken my axe and chopped a cord of wood from trees I'd felled and hauled then loaded it into the back of my truck to deliver to the hardware store in Cooper Valley.

Now, it was finally evening, the wood unloaded and

sold. I could see Summer again, according to the rules Rand set up for me.

He told me I had to give her space today. Wait for karaoke tonight at Cody's to see her again.

I did that. Now, I finally got to set eyes on Summer. Drink in her scent.

She wasn't working tonight, which meant I could steal her away afterward, if she'd let me.

But I had no idea if she'd be okay with us together two nights in a row.

The fact that Rand thought it necessary to drag me away from her this morning proved I didn't know what I was doing with her.

She was attracted to me. I knew that from the way she looked. The way her scent changed when I touched her. I knew I'd pleased her sexually. But she'd had some trauma, and Rand said I was coming on too strong. Cody'd said that, too. He had told me to let her lead.

I could do math equations in my head. I could argue the ethics behind genetic engineering. I could calculate the GDP of multiple foreign countries and the impacts that had on stock market fluctuations.

But I couldn't figure out what to do with Summer. How to act and talk, so I didn't scare her off. I felt... like an idiot.

"Fuck!" I shouted in the confines of my truck cab. I

was a shifter. A huge one. When my wolf finally scented his mate, I had to go against every instinct I had to keep her. It wasn't brains, it was biology.

I had to keep a chokehold on my wolf. Had to figure out how to be "chill" with her, as my brother would say.

I got out of the truck and scanned the lot for Summer's old beat-up Subaru. I didn't like her driving that thing. It was over fifteen years old and didn't have the latest safety features that kept humans protected in an accident. At least it was a good all-weather car and probably fairly dependable, but I was going to put her in something newer. An SUV, maybe, so she'd have room to drive our future pups around and make it up the mountain roads with ease.

Did she want pups? Did I? She said she was on the pill, but seeing my cum slip from her pussy made me think about how it would take some time to get her pregnant.

Fuck, I didn't care at this point if she wanted pups or not. I just wanted her, and practicing was sure as hell fun. We'd figure the rest out together, if I could just get us to be *together*.

I'd never wanted anything so much in my life.

Until now, I wasn't the kind of guy who needed people. After so long in New York, I preferred a solitary life out in the woods. I rarely went to pack meetings.

Occasionally hung out with my brothers. I'd resigned myself to most likely dying alone in my cabin, which, until last night, hadn't been a bad thing.

Now, Summer changed everything.

I would go moon mad and have to be put down if I didn't mark her eventually. But more than that, I suddenly wanted so much more out of my life.

I'd looked around my cabin today, trying to see it through her eyes and realized I was far too simple a man. It was one room with a loft and a bathroom. I'd built it from the logs I'd felled. The furniture was made by my brother. It was loaded with books. No TV. There was no lace or silk or anything softer than my comforter. I had nothing of interest for a young, vibrant mate. No doubt Summer would be bored or feel isolated. She'd think her life was *roughing it*. That wouldn't do. It was time to make some changes.

While my wolf knew Summer belonged to us, it didn't make a difference if I wasn't worthy of her. Maybe that was what Rand and Natalie were trying to point out.

I had a shit ton of money. I had a home. I could take care of Summer.

But could I make her happy? It was time to use that money to make changes and make the cabin more than shelter. To make it a home for both of us.

Meeting Summer made me realize I'd been too

isolated. I definitely needed to get out more. To reconnect with my pack instead of avoiding social gatherings altogether. To find a hobby besides reading books on military blockades of the War of 1812 and the entomology of the ash boring beetle, chopping wood, and building log cabins.

I tucked my clean flannel shirt into my jeans and walked up the wooden steps to Cody's Saloon. It was Sunday, so things were much slower than they'd been last night. When I entered, I noticed there were just a smattering of regulars gathered around. A guy was up on the stage, singing off-pitch "Friends in Low Places" into the mic while the rest of the audience crooned along.

When I scented my mate, I spotted Summer sitting near the front with Natalie, Rand, and Cody's mate, whose name I forgot. Some of the other pack members were also there with their mates–Rob and Willow, Johnny and his new mate, whose name I also forgot. Fuck, I needed to be better connected to my pack. These women were human and would be great friends for Summer.

Summer looked over, as if she'd instinctively known I'd arrived, and my breath stalled in my chest. There was a lightness in her face that hadn't been there last time.

Because of me?

Fate, I hardly dared to hope so.

Maybe it was just from a good lay, and if that was the case, I'd take it. I had every intention of making sure my mate stayed satisfied in bed.

I strode right for her, weaving around the other tables and patrons, planning to ask permission to touch her again, but she'd stood and was already running my way.

Running.

And damn, she looked good. She wore a pair of cut-off jean shorts over black fishnet tights, black cowgirl boots, and a fuzzy turquoise cropped sweater.

Holy hell. She looked good enough to eat.

And I *definitely* planned on feasting.

I stopped moving, mesmerized. A smile crooked my lips. Part of me wanted to look behind me to make sure she wasn't running for someone else. But no, she was looking right at me.

I threw my arms open wide and waited.

She vaulted off one foot and threw herself at me, her legs wrapping around my waist.

I hooked my forearm under her ass and spun her around, inhaling her honey scent. Fuck, yes. This was what I'd been waiting for all day. I didn't want to put her down. In fact, I wanted to turn around and walk right out of the bar.

"Oh, baby. That was the best greeting a guy could

ever get." I kept spinning. "How'd you get so fucking sweet?"

She tipped her chin up, so our eyes met. "Miss me?" she chirped.

She was *definitely* lighter and brighter than she'd been last night. Even lighter and brighter than this morning, after the orgasms. And she was *really* glad to see me.

Maybe absence *did* make the heart grow fonder, as they said. Whoever *they* were clearly weren't shifters.

I thought a day apart just made me horny, veering close to insanity, but it must've been different for her. Except, she'd *run* for me. No one did that unless they really, really wanted the person. If she hated me, like I'd worried, she'd have run down the back hall and out the emergency exit.

"I missed you so fucking much I went a little crazy, and that's no exaggeration," I said, nuzzling her neck.

She laughed, smiling down at me, and I forced myself to grin back when I realized she thought it was a joke.

Right.

I was supposed to be giving her space.

Not smothering her.

Definitely not acting like I couldn't live an afternoon without her. Maybe I really was crazy.

"Just joking," I added. "Yep. Hyberbole."

"Oh, Boone," she breathed, and I was calmed by her saying my name.

I carried her back to the group, and she kicked her feet against my back with glee. "Permission to keep holding you like this all night?" I asked.

She laughed and pushed at my shoulders, and I reluctantly lowered her, so her feet touched the floor, still keeping contact with a hand on her hip.

"Does everyone here know Boone?" She presented me to the group gathered at the tables that were clustered in front of the stage. Last night, the space had been for dancing. Tonight, the place had more of a lounge vibe.

"Boone, good to see you." Rob stood and slapped me on the back then turned to the group. "This is my cousin. He and his brothers are like bears because they hole up on that mountain more than half the year, hibernating."

Damn. I was called out by my alpha, but because he was a straight shooter, he was only being honest.

It was true, and the pack always busted my balls for it, but in front of Summer, it suddenly felt like a fault I should've fixed by now. Except, I'd thought everyone would be safer if I stayed away. Rob Wolf included. He knew all about my father's keen interest in me becoming alpha in his place. How I'd almost killed him in a rage. Instead of being investigated by the Shifter Council, I'd gone to college and stayed away.

Now that I was back, it seemed Rob held no grudge. It sounded like he thought my isolation was a bad thing, but I'd done it for him. For everyone in the pack. But now that I had Summer–

I rubbed the back of my neck, feeling like the flaw was an obvious detriment to me *wooing* my mate.

She must've seen the misgiving on my face because she wrapped her arms around me from the side and squeezed. Fuck, that felt good. "I love a big, burly mountain man," she declared to the entire group, who probably were told that she was my mate.

My heart–and dick–seemed to swell and grow warm.

She loved a big, burly mountain man.

That meant me. ME.

She was probably just trying to make me feel better, but I filed the words away.

The guy singing on stage finished to a round of applause, and the emcee took the mic back. "Next up, we have Summer! Summer, what are you singing, doll?"

14

───────

SUMMER

Boone stiffened when the emcee called me *doll,* and I tensed, too, for a completely different reason, my stomach twisting. It seemed I'd been conditioned to avoid drama after all of Marty's hissy fits because if he'd been the one at my side and the guy had called my name, he'd have lost his shit.

He'd have thought I'd flirted with the guy, maybe even fucked him, to get a spot on the karaoke list. He'd have thought my outfit made me a slut. He'd have thought... all kinds of ridiculous shit that had brought my life to a standstill of low self esteem.

I looked up at Boone to catch his glower at the emcee. Felt the squeeze of his fingers at my waist.

Oh, God. He was looking at the emcee just like Marty would have. I felt a little queasy. I couldn't do this again. I swallowed hard, my mouth suddenly dry.

Then Boone's dark gaze swiveled to me, and his brows dipped in concern. "You okay, baby?"

"You're... you're not mad I'm going to sing? That I'm wearing this?"

It was his turn to frown as he took in every inch of me. "Mad? Hell, no. I can't wait to hear my girl. And that outfit? Hell, baby, what you do to me."

He can't wait...? He... he wasn't mad at me. I drew in a breath and exhaled. Okay.

He was the jealous possessive type, though. Would it turn into him blaming me, like Marty had, for the guy calling me *doll*? The emcee had called every woman who was brave enough to go on stage the same thing.

He turned to face me, tipped my chin up. "Are you nervous?" His voice had a coaxing tone. "Don't be. You're going to rock this." His grin was potent. My nipples tightened from just a look.

He thought I was nervous about singing. I wasn't. I'd been singing my whole life. When I first moved to town, Natalie had asked me to join the Barn Cats, the band she played fiddle with, but I turned her down, not even taking the time to consider it.

Marty had ruined music for me.

Marty ruined everything for me.

Ever since, Natalie had switched from nudging me to join the Barn Cats to begging and insisting I at least come to karaoke night instead. I'd only agreed to get her off my back. This morning, she'd called this my big night with Boone. Said he'd fall like a tree when he heard me sing.

She had a lot more faith in my talent than I did. No way could I take the knees out from a giant like Boone.

Her words though, true or not, had given me a little sip of my power back. I could remember how I used to hold the attention of a crowd. How I'd absorbed the energy, fed off it. I hadn't played big venues–just coffee shops and bars around town–but it had given me a chance to share my music. The songs I wrote.

I'd dreamed that some day I'd get a recording contract and perform on bigger stages.

But Marty made me believe I was a fool. Untalented. Or, only led to think I was talented because all people saw was me trying to be slutty.

Boone walked me toward the stage while I heard the Wolf Ranch group clapping and whooping for me. "I can't wait to hear you sing, baby," he rumbled as his hand tightened on my hip.

Another one of my in-my-head issues was gone. He didn't want to stop me from being the center of attention. It didn't bother him. In fact, he'd led me right up to perform. It wasn't a ding to his manhood although I wasn't sure if there was a more manly guy out there.

That was a good sign, too.

I took a deep breath, let it out.

Maybe this wouldn't be the disaster it had been starting to feel like. Maybe I could do this after all.

I climbed on the stage and took the mic from Joe, the emcee. "Thank you, Joe. And word to the wise, I think my date will tear your head off if you call me doll again."

I made it into a joke, even though half of me still felt queasy about it.

It worked. Joe looked sheepish and shrugged his shoulders. The crowd laughed, and everyone turned to look at Boone standing at the side of the stage.

He folded his arms across his massive chest. Whether he was playing along or dead serious was debatable.

"Whoa, Boone," Joe said, offering him a small wave. He obviously knew him, which made sense. It was a small town where everyone seemed to know everyone. "Sorry, man. I didn't know you were with Summer. No disrespect intended."

Boone inclined his head.

"Here's your song. Shania Twain, right, Summer?"

He turned to face Boone and the audience. "Not *doll*. She's definitely not someone I would ever call *doll* again." Joe didn't seem scared. He was playing it up for the crowd, and everyone laughed, and Boone's lips may have twitched.

I nodded, my hip bouncing to the music he'd already started up. It was "That Don't Impress Me Much," and I got really into it, having fun and singing my heart out.

Boone watched me, his jaw dropping, eyes lighting up when I hit a high note. I strutted around on the stage in my bootie shorts while the audience cat-called and whistled. Boone whistled the loudest. When I finished, he roared, throwing his meaty fists into the air like I'd just scored a touchdown for his favorite team.

"Thank you, everyone," I said into the mic before I handed it back, breathless and elated.

Boone came to the end of the stage to meet me.

"Catch me." I jumped into his arms again, and he caught me like I was a feather pillow. I didn't know what my fascination with climbing him was, but damn, it felt good. He was as big as a tree and just as sturdy, and I guessed it made me feel safe to jump off a ledge and know he'd be there to break my fall.

Or maybe it was just foreplay. Because straddling his hips *definitely* turned me on.

"Permission to keep holding you like this all night?" Boone tried again after kissing my breastbone and the side of my neck.

I laughed, not answering. He carried me back to the cluster of tables where our friends sat.

"You have the most incredible voice. Where'd you learn to sing?" He sank into a chair, keeping me straddled around his waist.

It was a lot of PDA, but no one seemed to mind.

In fact, all we got were encouraging smiles from everyone.

No one seemed to think Boone was a red flag. Natalie wasn't steering me away. None of the other women were. None of the men, either. Wouldn't the alpha of the pack prevent me from being with a pack member who was dangerous?

I should relax. Stop finding possible issues and just see where this was going between us. Boone wasn't Marty.

I wasn't the clueless twenty year old woman who fell for him either.

I was wiser. I knew my worth. My heart.

Natalie answered for me, since I was somewhere in la la land eyeing Boone. "Summer writes her own songs. She's a professional musician."

I felt the painful constriction in my chest around

talk of my music career. Or lack of. "No, I'm not," I said quickly. "I mean–I dabbled. Very past tense."

"Bullshit," Natalie said, picking up her pint glass. "She has massive talent, and it's only in the past because of your ex. It's time for you to shine, girlfriend!"

A young woman and her friends got up on the stage and started singing a terrible rendition of "Girls Just Wanna Have Fun." It was hard not to cringe, but they looked like they were having fun, and that was what music was about.

"You're opening for the Barn Cats tomorrow night. It's a done deal." Natalie fixed me with a stern look.

I hadn't agreed, yet, but she kept pushing me. Now, with Boone looking at me with encouragement–plus everyone around the table from Wolf Ranch–I caved. "Okay," I agreed.

Boone studied me. "I can't wait to hear more. Music is important to you." His brows drew together when he must have put some things together. "You give it up for him?" He asked in a low voice, and our friends looked away to give us privacy.

The surprise at having someone I'd only known for twenty-four hours call out my most painful secret made my stomach lurch up and lodge between my ribs. I glanced away.

Boone must've read the answer in my shocked

silence because a ripple of anger contorted his face. I felt a growl rumble in his chest.

It occurred to me that I should be scared–he truly looked terrifying when he was mad, but I somehow wasn't. Maybe it was because his arms tightened protectively around me. Maybe it was because I understood he was angry on my behalf.

"Yeah." I swallowed. How foolish I'd been. "Marty didn't like anything in my life that he thought was more important than he was," I admitted. I felt ashamed when I said it. My voice sounded wounded. It hurt to even speak the words although I'd hashed through as much with Natalie over the last couple of months. Every day I was in Cooper Valley, I thanked God for having a friend like Natalie, who gave me a place to live, hooked me up with a job, and helped me get back on my feet while I filed for divorce.

Boone's jaw clenched. "If he ever shows up here, I will rip his arms right off his body," he growled.

It was such a vivid image that I smiled although I suspected Boone might actually be capable of such a feat. Judging from what I saw when he tore the legs off the broken bed last night, he had superhuman strength.

I stroked his soft beard. He was such a grumpy, growly giant, and he wanted to be mine.

"You're more important than any man," Boone declared.

I stared at him. Did he mean himself included?

"Your talent is amazing, and I only heard one song. Your music is important to you. You're not gonna stop because some baby-man didn't get enough attention from you, are you?"

His characterization of Marty wrung a smile from me. Natalie had asked the same question, but I'd felt too discouraged, too defeated when she asked it. All I could think about was getting through the divorce and being rid of him for good. Earning enough money to pay off the lawyer and start paying rent to Natalie and Rand.

But the way Boone asked it made me feel brave. Like Marty was insignificant.

Was my music important? "I guess..." I tried to wrap my thoughts around the shame and pain that shrouded music. "I sort of feel like my music career was what trapped me with Marty."

I saw a little flicker in Boone when I said Marty's name, like he was cataloguing it and saving it for later. "What do you mean?"

I bit my lip then let the words out. "He convinced me to move in and marry him and that he'd support me while I focused on my career."

"I thought–" Boone's face darkened. "Then he did the opposite, he crushed your career."

It felt alarming to hear what happened described that way, but the tears that immediately sprang to my eyes said Boone was right–Marty had crushed my career.

But I had to admit my part in it, too. I gave a miserable shrug. "Yes. He thought I was flirting with everyone, like Joe. That if a guy like him called me *doll,* then I must've fucked him. That when I sang, they clapped only because I was dressed in slutty clothes. He said so many things that broke me, but I was the one who let him manipulate me into believing all of it. That our marriage took precedence."

Boone shook his massive head. "No. Don't blame yourself for his asshole manipulation. His only goal should've been to see you succeed. But instead it was to lock you up and cage you–" Boone trailed off, understanding dawning in his eyes. "Fuck. I came on way too strong this morning. I behaved just like your asshole ex." He rubbed his beard. "No wonder you needed space."

One of the walls I'd erected against Boone crumbled to the ground in that instant. He finally understood. He didn't gaslight me into thinking what he wanted was right.

"Baby, I'm sorry. I never meant to make you feel–"

he cut himself off again. "Yeah, I made you feel like a possession, didn't I?"

I sent him a relieved smile. "Well, you did keep calling me *yours*."

He didn't answer, but I could somehow feel the intensity of how much he truly *did* believe I was his. But I guessed the fact that he knew by my scent that I was "the one" for him made that clear.

"Remember, baby, while I said you're mine, I'm also yours. You get that?"

I never thought about flipping it around. Could I call Boone *mine,* too? Could I be just as possessive of him as he was of me? The idea of any woman in this bar setting their horny gaze on my man... okay, I kinda understood more.

But how did it work, exactly?

"What happens if your mate doesn't feel the same way?" I asked.

I saw a world of pain in his gaze. He rested his hands on my hips, his fingers holding fast, like he was afraid I'd run off. His throat worked. "I promised you I'd take no for an answer." His voice rasped out like a croak.

Oh, sweet man. "I'm not saying no," I reassured him. "I was just wondering how it works. Like, does a" –I dropped my voice to a whisper– "she-wolf ever say no?"

Boone's large hands squeezed my ass, pulling me closer on his lap. "Well, there's a strong biological urge. She couldn't deny that. But yeah, I mean, sometimes it doesn't work out." He looked like he was holding something back. Something I wouldn't like.

"Is there divorce?"

He nodded, still looking like he didn't want to tell me. "Yeah. I mean, it's not *divorce* like humans do, but a separation nonetheless. It's not common, but it can happen. It can be hard because a male's instinct is going to be to protect her, even if she doesn't want that protection."

Hmm. That sounded a little stalker-like. It also sounded a lot like Boone and me.

"Baby, I understand now I came on too strong," he repeated. "I'm probably gonna keep coming on too strong. That's just the way I am. But you need to know that you have sovereignty. You say no, I stop. Period. You say give me space, I give you space. Whatever you need to feel comfortable. But I promise you this–I will never, ever stand in the way of your career. I will never whine and bitch that you're not giving me enough when you shine so fucking bright. All I want is the honor of being your man. I wanna be the guy who makes you happy, keeps you safe, and keeps you screaming all night."

Everything in me turned to hot liquid at his words.

Marty never said anything like that to me. If he had, I wouldn't have believed him. But I believed Boone.

Suddenly, I was totally over karaoke.

"Well." I scooched in tighter over his lap, feeling the bulge of his cock through his jeans. "Let's get started on that third part, shall we?"

15

BOONE

I GROANED at the sensation of Summer rocking her sweet pelvis over my dick. I wasn't going to make it all the way to my home. I wasn't even going to make it to *her* home. I needed to taste my girl now. Right here at Cody's was going to have to do.

I stood up, keeping her legs wrapped around my waist.

"Later, I'm gonna take you home and show you what it means to be worshiped," I promised, meeting her stormy blue eyes. "But right now, I need to taste you, and it can't wait."

I carried her to the back of the bar, right into the storeroom. Cody would forgive me for what we were about to do in his space. He understood what it was like to have a mate you couldn't get enough of. I needed Summer with a desperation I couldn't control.

"What are we doing, Boone?" Summer giggled, glancing around.

Fuck, that sound. No fear, but joy.

"I just need to taste you, baby," I growled, my mouth watering. "I need to hear you call my name when you come. Then I'll be safe enough to drive you home. Or to my cabin if you wanna see it."

I gently set her feet down on the concrete floor and then dropped to my knees in front of her, unbuttoning her shorts. With my thumbs hooked in the waistband, I yanked them and her fishnets down to her knees.

She squealed. "Oh my God, Boone!"

I looked up at her with what I knew must be glowing with eyes. "You okay, baby? Permission to lick your pussy until you scream?"

The scent of her now was stronger. She was very aroused. Ready.

I held her thighs between my two hands, and I could feel them tremble with desire.

"P-permission granted." The pupils of her blue eyes were blown wide, and her skin was flushed a lovely peach pink.

Leaning forward, I licked into her, aggressively.

Fuck, yes. The scent. The taste.

Mine.

I went at that pussy like a starved man on his first meal in weeks. I sucked her labia into my mouth, laved her flesh with my tongue. I explored every millimeter of her sweet pussy, ending up at the clit.

She was dripping wet, her honey already soaking my beard. It was easy to shove one thick digit inside her.

She cried out, her fingers tangling in my hair, her ass and back hitting the beer boxes stacked against the wall.

"That's it, baby." I praised her as I pumped my finger in and out of her tight channel. Watching her from my knees was so powerful. I was giving her pleasure. She was taking it, trusting me with her body. "You look so pretty when you're ready to come." No, that didn't do her justice. "You are the most beautiful woman on the face of this earth."

That was fact.

I rolled my tongue over her clit and found her G spot on the inner wall inside her. I curled my finger to stroke it the way I'd learned the night before she liked as I licked, loving the way her panting cries grew more frantic.

"Like that, baby? Do you want it there?" I asked, making sure she guided me the way she wanted. I was her servant of pleasure.

"Yes! Yes, Boone, right there." Her voice bounced off the concrete walls of the small room.

I added a second finger and pumped them, angling my hand, so the pads of my fingertips hit that G spot every time.

She screamed, grabbing my wrist to hold my hand still as she gushed fluid around it. "Oh, oh!" Her walls clenched in a quick pulsing action, squeezing and spasming around my fingers.

"That's it, baby. Good girl. I love it when you come for me."

She grew even wetter, as if my praise turned her on. I made a mental note to make sure I praised the fuck out of her every chance I got. I was cataloguing everything that made her happy. Made her wet. Made her come.

Hell, every fucking thing about her.

I eased my fingers out and put them in my mouth, savoring the taste of her juices. I couldn't get enough.

Carefully, I pulled up her fishnet tights then her shorts, zipping and buttoning them. Then I stood, leaned down so I could nuzzle her neck. "I fucking love making you come," I breathed in her ear then bit it. "Will you come home with me tonight?"

"Yes," she answered immediately. No hesitation. No fear. Thank fuck.

"I want you to sing for me again," I said. "Naked and from my bed. My own show."

The slow smile she gave me had a wicked tinge to it that made my balls throb. "Okay."

I grabbed her hand and led her out of the storeroom. Her taste on my tongue, a smile on her face.

I thought last night was the best night of my life. But tonight was turning out even better.

16

SUMMER

I PULLED on one of Boone's flannels. A bright red and so soft. It was so big, I didn't even button it. Boone's cabin was incredible. It had been dark when he brought me here last night after stopping at my place, so I could pack a bag. We drove high up in the mountains from town. When we arrived, we'd been–er, *busy* until I pretty much passed out from pleasure–but now in the light of morning, I looked around.

I'd call it cozy-luxury, if that was a thing. Last night, he told me he'd built it all himself. It clearly was a labor of love.

It was small–a studio cabin with an open living room/kitchen/bedroom area and a loft which he appeared to use as an office/library. While rustic, every detail was perfection. The heavy wooden doors featured engraved designs and fit snugly against the harsh winter. The cabinets and drawers in the kitchen all had the finest hardware and the soft-close feature. Invisible lights under the cabinets cast a glow on the gorgeous countertops. Both the kitchen and bathroom counters and shower walls were giant slabs of polished quartz–white and grey, with veins of purple and silver.

The pale wood floors were smooth and felt soft and welcoming. A cast-iron woodstove kept the place warm.

Natalie had said Boone was really smart–that he'd gone to college at age sixteen–but I really hadn't pegged him as a bookworm. He wasn't one for saying much, and with me, he'd stuck his foot in his mouth half the time. Yet the entire cabin was packed with books that he'd clearly read.

Every wall of the upstairs loft featured shelves, and one entire wall downstairs was also chock full of books. I ran my fingertips along the spines of some, scanning them. They covered everything–trade wars with China, the AI revolution, ancient Egyptian religion, craftsmen's books on woodworking and construction, German philosophy, Jungian psychology.

"Wow," I murmured. "You like to read."

Boone was in bed, his large head propped on his

hand as he lay on his side watching me. He shrugged, causing his muscular shoulder to ripple with muscle. "It gets boring up here in the winter," he said simply.

I returned to the bed and crawled on top of him, straddling his thick trunk. He could easily flip me and dominate me, but he didn't. His flannel hung over my shoulders like an open robe. "Why do you live up here all by yourself?"

There was something about Boone's living situation that felt like he was guarding against something. Not hiding, necessarily, but isolating by choice.

He hesitated, which told me I was onto something. His dark eyes looked troubled. "It's just... safer this way," he muttered, looking away.

"Safer for whom? For you?"

He shook his head. A deep furrow creased a line between his eyes.

I cocked my head. "What aren't you telling me?"

His jaw clenched. He hadn't moved his giant body, but I could feel the tension pulsing through him.

"Please, I want to know. What happened? Did you... did you hurt someone? Your wolf did?" I wasn't sure what made me guess that, but I immediately knew I was right by the way his eyes popped wide in surprise.

He stopped breathing.

"You can tell me, Boone," I whispered, my finger

running through the dark hair on his chest. The sleeves of his flannel were so long I couldn't see my hands.

He didn't speak.

I hadn't known him long, but I knew enough. "I know you're afraid of scaring me off. I guess I am kind of skittish. But I need to know everything about the man who says he's my mate."

Wow. Saying those words out loud affected me.

The man who says he's my mate. It was like I could feel the tug of fate behind the words. The heavy meaning Boone and the rest of my friends attached to the word, *mate.*

Boone slowly released his breath. He stared up into my face like it was a lifeline. Like he could see right into my soul. He cleared his throat. "Growing up, my uncle–my mother's brother–was alpha of this pack." His voice sounded rusty.

I wanted to ask if he meant Rob's dad, but I waited, letting him take his time to tell the story the way he wanted to tell it.

"My mom died while giving birth to Roy. My dad was... what you think of when people say 'toxic masculinity.' But my aunt and uncle–Rob's, Colton's and Boyd's parents–looked out for us when we were kids. Or pups, as we say. They were the loving parents we wished we had." He drew in another breath and released it. "When I was sixteen, they were killed in a terrible car crash in the canyon. Rob was young–just a couple of years older than I was. The leadership of the pack fell to him, as expected."

I nodded, still lightly running my fingernails through the hair on his strong chest, trying to soothe away the pain I could read on his face. He was so warm beneath me.

"I was big already–I was this tall by middle school, and in high school I'd filled out. My asshole dad thought I should challenge Rob to be alpha."

I raised my brows in surprise but, otherwise, didn't interrupt, especially since I didn't know what that exactly meant.

He sighed. "I know–it was ridiculous. My father was a selfish, scheming prick. I had no interest in leadership or in taking something away from the cousin who was like a brother to me, who'd actually been raised to take over and lead. I just wanted out of my house. I wanted to get away from my dad and his constant pressure on me to perform as an alpha male. To you, a human, that means being dominant and in charge, but an alpha of a wolf pack is that and more. He's the leader, the one completely responsible for everyone's wellbeing. Plus, he metes out justice, at least at pack level. He has to make decisions that sometimes aren't positive or happy.

I could've filled the role with my size, but that was it. It was *in* Rob to be alpha. He was born to follow his father. Mine believed my size made me born to lead, and that was why he was a dick. I wasn't qualified."

"Like forcing a square peg in a round hole?" I guessed.

The corner of his mouth tipped up. "Yeah, like that. Rob fit the role. I didn't. I'd studied my ass off to graduate high school early and go to college. I'd already been accepted to Columbia. But my dad wouldn't let up. For months, he was on me about it. Challenge, challenge, challenge. One night that summer, he pushed me too far, and we fought. Not verbally but physically. I didn't mean to challenge *him* for dominance–it just happened."

I had no idea what *challenge for dominance* meant, but Boone's eyes had lost their focus, and his expression looked sickened. Whatever he did, he regretted it to this day.

"What happened?" I whispered.

I watched guilt wash over Boone's face. "It was bad." He swallowed.

I waited, but he didn't go on.

"How bad?"

His hands settled on my hips, his thumbs stroking my skin, but I doubted he even knew he was doing it.

"A fucking bloodbath. I mean–my wolf didn't kill my father, but it was close."

When he saw my look of alarm, he quickly amended, "Shifters heal fast, though. He was fine. But Roy and Ace, my other younger brother, were totally traumatized. I–" He stopped speaking, like the words had choked him. "I left. The pack, the state. I probably should've stayed. For them. But I'd almost beaten my father to death. I figured with me gone, the threat to everyone would be gone, too. Also, it would be better for Rob trying to run the pack at a young age, and for peace in the family if I left town and stayed gone. I didn't want to be the violent one everyone was worried about erupting again.

"So I went to college, and then I stayed in New York after I got my degree. I told myself I was allowing Rob the space to secure his leadership. Later, I told myself working as a hedge fund manager was about making money for the family, and I *did* make money. A ton of it. That's how we started the tree farm and bought all this land back from the bank."

My hands stilled and one rested over his heart. I felt the slow beat of it beneath my palm. "Were your brothers in danger?"

The pain in Boone's expression gutted me.

I cradled his face and stroked his silky beard with my thumbs.

He shook his head but wouldn't meet my eyes. "No... not physical danger. But our dad was a narcissist–so they didn't get the support they deserved. Fortunately, Rob didn't oust them from the pack or remove his protection, even though he had to know my dad had been scheming for his position. But Roy and Ace lost the love and stability of our aunt and uncle when they died, and Rob wasn't equipped to be a surrogate parent for them anymore than I was. Things came to a head five years after I left when my dad tried to get Ace to challenge Rob. Ace had no interest, never even considered the role. He wasn't the first-born of our family, and Rob has two younger brothers. If anyone was going to replace Rob, it'd be Colton then Boyd. Because of this attempt, Rob banished him from the pack."

My eyes widened. Who knew there was so much drama in a wolf pack? I guessed people who knew wolf packs existed in the first place.

"He banished Ace?"

"No, my dad, not Roy and Ace. Our dad left the state. Last we heard, he was in a pack in Arkansas. That was the best thing that could've happened, really, because my brothers stayed and finally had their freedom."

"They live up here on the mountain, too, right?" I

remembered what he said. One of them was a woodworker, and the other had a Christmas tree farm.

He nodded.

"Is that when you came home? When your dad was banished?"

Boone grimaced. "I should have but no."

"What brought you back?"

"Some more trouble. Not here at the pack but in New York." I sensed Boone close off, like he didn't want to tell me any more. It hurt to be pushed away, especially when he had just opened up so well.

I tried to keep the connection open. "You may have been big and smart, but you were still just a kid when you left. Sixteen is young to go to college, especially one in New York after living in Cooper Valley. You can't be blamed for your dad's shitty parenting or for not wanting to stay and somehow make things better for your brothers. I imagine you were right—staying would've meant more fights and problems."

Boone let out a long exhale. "Thanks. My brother, Ace, doesn't feel that way, but it helps to hear you think so." His voice was rough. "Come here." He pulled me down to rest my head on his chest and hugged me to him. He was so warm, his skin soft over hard muscle.

I snuggled over him, offering comfort in the form of my presence. "Thank you for sharing. I'm sorry you had to go through that."

He stroked his large, calloused hands down my bare back and lightly circled my ass. "I don't want you scared of me." His voice cracked a little. "I know something happened to you. I will never, ever let you get hurt again. I promise you that." His voice had turned fierce, and I knew without a shadow of a doubt that he could be violent again. But I also believed it would not be with me, only to protect me.

Hearing what happened and his guilt over leaving his brothers made me sure of it. He had a sense of honor. His moral compass was intact. I didn't know anything about wolf shifters, but I did understand the concept of alphas. He may not want a leadership position, but he was a natural leader. Dominant. Protective. Willing to use force when necessary. Yet he'd left his pack to ensure Rob's leadership as alpha was successful.

I was sure that must have been scary for a sixteen-year-old, but it wasn't a reason to keep himself isolated up here on the mountain now. If we were going to be a couple—a thought that half-excited, half-terrified me—then I would have to draw him back into society. I knew from experience how awful it was to be cut off from your support system and community. How scary it was to try to reengage.

I saw his fear of this around me. He was afraid to do something wrong. He felt like he would step wrong, say something wrong, *do* something wrong to hurt me or scare me away. I couldn't get a read of my own fear with him turning into Marty–being super nice and sweet to start and then turning controlling and mean. I had to work on it.

I could start now.

I smiled slyly, thinking of a *very* good idea.

"I want to tie you up."

His eyes flared wide then heated. "I assume you mean here in bed," he said. His voice had dropped an octave, and every hint of guilt and regret slipped from his gaze.

I bit my lip and nodded. "I want to have my way with you."

"You afraid I'm going to hurt you?" he asked, suddenly wary again.

I shook my head. "No. Not at all. I want you to let go. To forget about trying to not hurt me. I know that goes through your head."

He nodded once.

"This way, you know you can't. You can let go and just... enjoy."

"So you're gonna fuck yourself on me? Drive me fucking crazy with that sweet pussy?"

He reached up, slid his flannel from my shoulders, so it pooled around my hips. I pulled my arms from the sleeves, and I was naked. His gaze roamed over me, and his dick swelled between us.

I nodded.

"I'm all for it, but you gotta do something first."

I cocked my head, my hair brushing my jaw. "What?"

"After you tie me up, you gotta sit on my face. I'm gonna eat that sweet pussy until you come. My girl comes first, and this way I know that's happened."

Did I want to do that? Have Boone eat me out and come for him *then* ride him like a cowgirl?

Yes, yes I did.

"Okay."

"Good." He raised his hands over his head and gripped the hewn wood headboard. "Use my flannel to tie my wrists to the wood."

I did as he instructed, leaning forward to wrap the sleeve around his wrists and the slat, but he latched onto one of my nipples, and I got distracted.

Finally, he was secure, and I was really turned on.

He grinned, looked up, and gave the knot a test tug.

"Climb on up here, baby."

I shimmied up his torso then grabbed hold of the top of the headboard and settled my knees on either side of his head.

"Lower down. Yes, fuck. Good girl."

Then he ate me out with a ruthless precision.

Perhaps it was because he was determined for me to come first that he didn't tease or taunt. He couldn't use his hands, but his mouth and tongue were so talented, I came in record time. If there was speed pussy eating in the Olympics, Boone would definitely win Gold.

I was wilted and sated but not done. That orgasm had been a warm-up. His dick was behind me, thick and long and dripping pre-cum. His belly was coated in it.

"Ready?" I asked, which was ridiculous. He was beyond ready. He grinned, his beard was shiny, covered in my arousal.

I shifted back, came up on my knees, then sank onto him.

"Fuck," he hissed, tugging at the knot. It held.

I felt very powerful having a guy like Boone at my mercy.

"Just feel, baby," I told him, leaning down and kissing him, tasting myself on his lips.

I pushed up, began to move then.

"Cup those tits," he said.

I did, and I felt him swell inside me.

Then I set my hands on the headboard and leaned over, giving him one to suck. Then the other.

I was moaning and writhing on his dick but had to sit back up. I wanted more. Harder. Deeper. I took it.

Used Boone's dick to make myself come. Watched his face–clenched jaw, flushed cheeks, wild eyes.

"You gonna come for me, big guy?" I asked, riding him.

"Yes. So close."

"Come for me, Boone. Just let go."

Maybe he needed the words. Maybe I'd pushed him to the point of no return.

He thrust his hips up and came on a growl, filling me with his cum until it slipped out around him. I needed more. I reached down, rubbed my clit and pushed myself over the edge again. It felt so good with him thick and hard inside me.

I'd reduced this big lumberjack, who was so strong, to a sweaty, sated mess.

I grinned. So did he.

I leaned forward to kiss him, his skin so hot against mine. "Thank you."

He laughed. "Baby, you can tie me up anytime."

Now, being caught in a snowstorm in the mountains with Boone didn't feel like a trap. It felt exciting.

BOONE

Having Summer in my cabin was an ecstatic experience. It also was pure torture because her honey and peaches scent filled the small space, continually riling up my wolf. He wanted non-stop sex with her. He needed to hear her scream. Feel her orgasm. Smell her arousal.

Most of all, he wanted to mark her. Especially when she'd tied me up and had her way with me. Fuck, that had been hot.

But I hadn't figured out how to broach the topic of claiming with her. I'd moved too fast before. Now that I understood she had triggers, I had a choke collar on my wolf. When she'd suggested me being restrained while we fucked, I'd thought it had been a good idea–after she explained she hadn't been afraid. I could be assured I wasn't too rough. She could take what she wanted, and I sure as hell was going to come from whatever she did.

It was a start. She was so strong and brave, and it had shone through as she rode me to the most impressive orgasm of my life.

But claiming? That still had to happen. The clock was ticking. Time was running out for me not to go moon mad. I could feel the chaotic energy simmering within me. The animal warring with the man. I was hot and agitated. On edge. Like I had too much energy running through my body for my skin to contain.

She stood and pulled on her clothes. For a moment, I lay on the bed to watch because there was nothing more beautiful in this world than my mate. Also, because I needed to calm my wolf, who freaked out just because she climbed off of me. After what she just did to me, I could've been sated but no.

This was getting to be a problem. She might have protected herself by tying me up, letting me forget about possibly harming her. But it was back now with a vengeance. I would never forgive myself if I ended up losing control and putting her in danger like I promised would never happen. Or marking her before she was ready. I forced him back down.

I rolled to get up and pulled on a pair of sweats. "You must be hungry after that." I winked at her, and she blushed prettily. "I have sausage and eggs. I could probably figure out pancakes, too. There's real maple syrup. And coffee. Of course, I have coffee. Or hot cocoa."

She smiled at me, and something shifted in my chest. I wanted to make this woman happy more than I cared about my next breath. But what if I was still a danger to her? I knew my wolf would never intentionally let anything happen, but if I were protecting her, fate knew I wouldn't be able to hold back the violence. And then I might lose her anyway.

"Eggs and sausage sound great. And if you have chocolate let's make mochas!" She bounced a little on her feet.

Fuck, she was cute.

I started the coffee and pulled out a skillet while she opened the refrigerator and found the eggs and sausage.

Fifteen minutes later, we sat down to heaps of steaming food with mugs of coffee with milk and hot cocoa mix.

"You must think I can eat like a wolf," Summer laughed, picking up her fork and eyeing the huge mound of eggs and sausage.

My wolf loved providing for her.

I grinned. Fuck, I didn't know my face even knew how to smile anymore, but apparently, it remembered. "You need your energy if we're going on a mountain hike in the snow to see the tree farm."

She chewed her bite of food, smiling at me in a way that made my entire world crumble and rearrange itself.

Claim her. My wolf wouldn't stop.

I forced him back down. *Not. Yet. Soon.*

"Which brother did you say owns the tree farm? Will I get to meet him?"

"Ace. Uh, sure. You want to?" My chest felt too tight. Like it was expanding, and my ribs couldn't contain the energy.

"Of course, I do."

I held still for a moment. Was it possible she was already accepting me as her mate? Wanting to meet my family was a good sign, right?

"I'll make you a deal."

She smiled, lifting her brows. "What deal?"

"I'll show you the tree farm if you sing a song for me. One of your songs. Maybe an original one that you wrote?"

Summer flushed. "Well, yeah." She let out an embarrassed laugh. "Okay. I'll sing the whole way, if you want."

"I want." I held her gaze. "I want to hear every

beautiful thing you wrote. Now that I know how good you are, I'm gonna make sure you don't abandon yourself or your music for a man again."

Tears sprang into her eyes. "Boone." Her voice scratched.

I immediately pushed back from the table to make room and held my arm out to her. "Come here, baby."

She surged up from the table and came to me, and I pulled her onto my lap, wrapping one arm around her waist and kissing her shoulder.

"I won't smother you, Summer. I promise. I know I come on too strong. I'm too intense. My wolf wants to claim you, and I want to protect you, but I'm not gonna keep you to myself. I mean, if you let me have you."

Her arms twined around my neck, and she kissed my head. She didn't agree. Didn't say she believed me or trusted me, but I could somehow feel that the tying up sex and this, they were a start. I was making progress. I would find out all her objections and fears and make sure I addressed them. Eventually, she'd believe she was completely safe with me.

"We might be up in the mountains here, but I would never try to keep you from the world. Just hearing you sing karaoke, and I know that you were born to be enjoyed by the masses, baby. And I know it's probably too soon to say this, but I just want to get it all out in the open. If you think it's too remote up here, I'll buy or build a place in town. Your happiness is what matters to me."

"Christ, Boone," she choked. "Quit making me cry."

"If you're crying because you feel worshipped like you deserve, I won't apologize."

She let out a watery chuff. "You're crazy."

I stood, holding her in my arms, and she instinctively wrapped her legs around my waist. "Yup." I kissed her. "Crazy about you."

18

SUMMER

Coming from Los Angeles, I didn't think I could handle the winter in Montana, but over the past few months, I had fallen in love with snow. Boone and I headed out into it with woolen hats and down parkas. I had a pair of Boone's thick wool socks on to keep my feet warm even if they got wet.

I couldn't see any paths or roads, but Boone led the way through the forest like he knew exactly where he was going, holding my mittened hand in his.

Part of me wondered if this was dangerous—whether we could get hypothermia or lose our way, but then I remembered that Boone was a wolf. They didn't get lost in the woods, did they?

Damn, that was hot. He wasn't just a gorgeous lumberjack genius, but he was superhuman. He probably had better hearing and sense of smell. And, of course, he could change into a giant wolf. Oh!

"I want to see you in wolf form," I blurted, standing amongst the trees, the snow falling lightly.

He tipped his head down to look at me, his eyes crinkling. "Yeah?"

Flakes fell on my face and melted. "Yeah. Do you only change during the full moon?"

He shook his head. "No. We can shift anytime. The full moon just makes us itchy to shift. It's like... seeing a tray of fresh baked cookies and grabbing one. They'd be hard to resist."

That made sense. "What... um, color are you? Your um, fur."

"White and silver. I definitely blend in on a snowy day."

"Blend in? You mean, to hunt? What do you hunt?" I wasn't sure if I should be grossed out or not.

He smiled again. "What do I hunt? Little blonde musicians who sing like angels." Boone suddenly lunged for me, swooped me up in the air, and spun me around, his heat seeping through my layers.

I whooped and giggled.

He set me down on my feet, a grin on his face.

"You'd better run, babygirl." His voice held mock warning.

I laughed, taking off running, snow kicking up all around me. I twisted to look over my shoulder, and my breath came out in a big cloud.

Damn him!

He didn't even need to run, his long strides kept him right behind me.

"This isn't even hard for you, is it?" I called, breathless. I ran faster, tripping over a tree root under the snow and flying headlong into a snowdrift.

I faceplanted in the fluffy, soft snow.

"Ack!" It was freezing!

It got under the bottom hem of my jacket and down by my throat. In the space between my gloves at my sleeves and my wrists. I was only down for a second, though, because Boone instantly scooped me up out of the cold and into his arms.

"Whoops. You okay, baby?" Boone's warm brown gaze traveled over my face with concern as he brushed the snow from me.

"Yes. I am now." I leaned up and kissed his chin. His cold cheeks. His soft lips framed by the scratchy beard.

I loved the way I felt cared for with him. Marty would've laughed at me falling down. Taken it as his victory in the race. Or worse, called me clumsy. And of course, he couldn't just pluck me up from the ground and into his arms like I weighed nothing, like Boone just did. No matter what he thought of himself, he wasn't that strong.

"Ahh, I see." Boone started walking, still carrying me as he continued on. "This was just your ploy to be carried on this hike."

I laughed. "No. I can hike."

He shook his head, a smile tipping up the corner of his mouth. "No chance, beautiful. You're in my arms now, and I'm not putting you down. So pay your way with a song."

Pay my way with a song.

I laughed. We were out in the middle of nowhere. Nothing but trees and mountains and snow all around. "Okay. You have to imagine it with my guitar, too."

"I want to hear it *a cappella*. Just your perfect voice, like you're gonna do tonight at the concert. And when we get home, I'm going to strip you naked, fuck you thoroughly, and put my guitar in your hands to hear it that way, too."

If any part of me had been cold from the snow or brisk air, I was heated thoroughly now. I squirmed in his arms, turned on by his promise. Turned on by his interest in my music. Turned on by all the attention he showered on me that actually didn't feel smothering at all. It just felt... well, attentive.

I drew in a breath, listening to imaginary guitar chords in my head to count me in. Then I sang one of my slower songs–a moody piece I'd written about a rainy day and unrealized dreams.

Boone didn't even watch where he was going. His gaze was trained on my face with rapt attention. Wonder, even, as I sang to him.

When I finished, he slowly lowered me to the ground. "By the moon, did you write that yourself?"

I nodded, feeling my cheeks heat with pleasure.

"Summer, it's incredible." He shook his head with... wonder? "You have to sing that one tonight. How do you not have a recording contract?" His look changed to determination. "We're going to get you a recording contract."

I let out an incredulous laugh. "We are? Just like that?"

"Yeah. I know someone in the biz. A former client. I can reach out. Do you have samples or a demo tape or whatever they call it?"

I blinked. We were in the *woods,* and he was making all these plans? It seemed like his big brain got working on an idea and ran with it. "Um. No. I mean, I did, but Marty has my computer. They weren't real ones, anyway. I'd need to go into a real sound studio to record, and he said..." I broke off, feeling queasy.

"He said what?" Boone growled, brushing a finger over my cold cheek. He didn't even need gloves.

Anger flooded through me. I'd believed that asshole. Now, with the distance of a few months and living with people who cared about me, I could see it was all part of his manipulation.

"He said I wasn't ready."

"Like he's some fucking judge?" Boone scoffed.

"Right? He was just an asshole cop who liked country music."

Whoops. I could see the intelligence behind Boone's eyes as he cataloged the fact that I'd shared that Marty was a cop. I needed to be careful not to encourage his desire to exact revenge on Marty, as flattering as it might be.

"That song is ready," he said. "You're ready. People need your music. We'll get you a contract, and the world will never be the same." He stopped and rotated, so I could see where he pointed. "There are the trees."

I followed his finger to see a vast expanse of small pine trees, planted in neat rows.

"Are these the babies?" I asked.

"Not saplings, but you're right, they are too small still to sell. These trees are about three years old. They'll be ready in another three." He lowered me to my feet, took my hand, and led me down a hill. On our right side spanned another large grid of trees. It was clear these were planted in comparison to the natural forest we'd walked through from his cabin. "This lot is four years old. The trees that are ready for this year are down a bit further." He pointed in the direction of two log cabins, larger than his, with smoke coming out of the chimneys. "That's where Ace and Roy live. The larger house is where we grew up and Ace lives there. The building in the back is Roy's place, which also has his woodworking studio."

I glanced up at him to read his expression. His two brothers lived together but Boone had chosen to build his cabin far apart from them. Apart from everyone.

"Do you not get along?"

Boone's expression was wooden. He shrugged. "I abandoned them when they needed me most. So yeah, there are some hard feelings. But we still take care of each other."

I had no brothers or sisters, but still, grief slid through me for him. I could feel his guilt and regret, and I wanted to rip it from him. Give him a chance for a fresh start. With his brothers. With the pack. With me.

With me.

That felt right.

I was his fresh start. If I were to believe what he said—and honestly, I was starting to—then he was willing to make changes. It sounded like he didn't need me to be the only one who had to contort and pretzel herself to stay in the relationship. It felt like we could actually be partners.

Or was that just what he said to lock me in? Would I turn into a possession once he married me or mated me or whatever they did?

We walked through the grove of trees toward the buildings. It felt magical–the soft snow falling on our heads, the green pine peeking out from beneath the heavy coat of white that shrouded them, as I held Boone's hand.

For the first time in years, I started to compose a song in my mind.

Snow falling on pines.

Your hand held in mine.

There's no better time

than this one.

I followed the creative thread, letting it play in my head, already knowing the notes I'd sing.

Was it a sign that the first song I'd composed in years came right after I met Boone?

It felt like a good omen. Boone had inspired me. He made me feel safe and–God, I hoped–would give me the space I needed to be creative.

"You okay?" he asked. "You're quiet down there."

"Down here?" I laughed, tipping my head back to

meet his dark eyes. "I'm not that short! But yes, I'm good. I'm working on a song in my head."

He cocked his head, and his lips twitched with amusement. "Yeah? Awesome. I can't wait to hear it."

We'd reached the closer cabin now, and Boone hesitated before he pounded on the door then pushed it open.

Two men, both as large and imposing as Boone, looked over from the dining room table, where something like furniture sketches had been spread.

No one said hello. They just stared at us.

"Hey guys. This is Summer. My mate."

19

BOONE

As I shut the door behind us, Ace and Roy unfolded themselves from their chairs and stood, staring at Summer in wary surprise. Roy's nostrils flared as he took in her scent.

He sent me a shocked look, and I narrowed my gaze.

Yeah, she was human, asshole. So what? I growled, tightening my arm around her.

Summer stiffened, looking up at me.

Right. Growling might scare her. Especially when she didn't know why the fuck I was doing it.

"You mated?" Ace asked. Ace was two years younger, a few inches shorter, and many pounds lighter. Which meant he was big and really fit, but not a giant like me. He kept his dark hair cut short, and the same went with his beard. He was quick to smile although it was rarely aimed at me. Fortunately, he offered one to my mate as he walked forward and held out his hand for her to shake. "When? Why didn't you tell us?"

I shrugged. "It just happened."

"Did you get lost in the woods, sweetheart?" Roy asked. He was the baby but bigger than Ace. He kept his hair long, skimming his jaw, which he often pulled back, like it was now. He didn't have a beard, but he easily delayed a few days between shaves. "I'm Roy, by the way." He shook Summer's hand next.

This was the house I grew up in. I didn't like coming to the place. It was where my worst memories were. But in the years since our father was banished, Ace cleared out all evidence of the man and made changes. Updates. Fresh paint. A modern kitchen, and today, the scent of beef and garlic wafted from the crockpot on the granite counter. New furniture that Roy built. It became something different, but it was hard to let go of the past.

"Hi. Um, no. Why?" she asked.

"'Cause big brother doesn't leave the mountain," Roy explained.

"We met at Cody's. I'm a cocktail waitress there," she told them.

Their eyes widened on me. "You went to Cody's?" Ace asked, stunned.

Summer glanced between us, and I rubbed the back of my neck, suddenly feeling like something as simple as going to a bar on a Saturday night was so crazy. Or maybe I was. "Yeah."

"Hell. We can't even get you to go to a pack meeting with us, and you were all the way in town," Ace said, shaking his head. He looked to Summer. "Our brother is a little shy. Doesn't like crowds."

She laughed then glanced at me. It wasn't a teasing look, instead, gentle. "Oh, I know. We're working on that, but I got him to go to karaoke even."

My brothers' mouths fell open. "Karaoke? Seriously? Did a tree fall and hit you on the head when you were chopping it down?" Roy asked, grinning. Ace crossed his arms and laughed.

He was kidding with me, but it still stung a little. "If finding my mate is the same as getting hit on the head by a tree, then yeah. Shoulda done it sooner if it led me to Summer."

My brothers appeared flabbergasted. I didn't blame them. I didn't have much excitement in my life, and in the past few days since I'd seen them last, a lot had happened.

"Wow, Summer. You're a great influence for our brother," Roy commented.

With that, I agreed.

"Why don't you join us tonight?" she offered. "We're going... I mean, I'm the opening act for the Barn Cats in Missoula. I, um... sing."

"Sing?" I said. "Baby, don't make yourself small." I glanced at my brothers. "She's an artist. A songwriter. Her voice is amazing, and I'm not biased at all because she's my mate. Natalie thinks so. The rest of Wolf Ranch who were there last night thought so, too."

Their eyes widened. I wasn't sure if it was because they were impressed that Summer was so talented or because I was raving about a woman. And that I'd been in town. At Cody's. Twice. And I'd found my mate.

Lots of shocks at one time.

I barely stopped by to visit them unless we were talking business or Ace made his famous chili.

"She's gonna be a fucking star," I told them, and Summer blushed. I wrapped an arm around her and kissed the top of her head. "Come listen, and you'll agree."

Ace and Roy glanced at each other.

"Wouldn't miss it," Ace said.

Roy nodded. "Pick us up on the way into town. Maybe we'll find our mates next."

20

SUMMER

BEING up on stage again felt amazing. I didn't know why I was reluctant to return to performing, when it was as natural to me as breathing. The lights. The crowd. All of it.

As I sang my third song on the stage of Boondocks, a large country bar / music venue in Missoula, I looked out at the throng and drank in their energy. My friends were settled up close to the stage. We'd driven over in Boone's big truck with Ace and Roy, caravaning with Natalie, Rand, and the rest of our friends.

Boone sat front and center, flanked by his brothers. All three of them were stacked with muscles and wore a protective air, like they were my bodyguards. Natalie and her bandmates were there as well, along with Rand, Cody, Riley, Rob, Willow, Colton, Marina, Johnny, and Emma.

I wore an outfit Natalie helped me pick out–a pink denim skirt with black fishnets, black boots, and a black crop top. I wore my black cowgirl hat with the pink band that matched my skirt. Unlike in LA, I blended right in here in Montana.

I finished the last note, and the crowd went nuts. It was a Monday night, so I didn't think anyone would show up to hear us play, even in a larger city, but the place was packed, and the men in particular were going crazy for me–whistling and yelling for more.

A drunk guy wandered up close to the stage. "Play a song for *me*, sweetheart." He ducked his head like he was trying to look up my denim mini skirt.

A note of anxiety pinched under my ribs, and I flubbed the next line and had to restart. This could go badly. Would Boone start a fight? Would he blame me for this guy's behavior? How ugly would this get?

I had at least a dozen bad memories of scenes just like this with Marty getting nasty when I drew attention from men. I remembered the event itself and then the repercussions for days afterwards.

Boone was already on his feet, his large form moving with cat-like grace. "Stay away from my girl, buddy." He hauled the guy back with a heavy hand on his shoulder, rotating him, and giving him a shove to send back in the direction he'd come from.

When Boone turned back around after ensuring the guy wouldn't bother me any longer, he winked at me.

Winked.

He wasn't mad. He had my back. Warmth spread through my chest. I sighed, letting out a breath I hadn't realized I'd been holding.

My wolf-man was protective. Possessive, even. But he didn't seem to blame me for the attention I got, the way Marty had.

I finished up the song with a renewed feeling of... freedom and bowed my head to their applause. I couldn't stop grinning. God, it felt amazing! "Thank you all so much. Now, I think it's time to turn the stage over to the Barn Cats," I said.

"Sing another song!" some guy yelled from the back.

"One more song," another began to chant. Others joined in and even added feet stomping to their eagerness.

When I realized that even Natalie and the rest of the Barn Cats were chanting, I laughed and ran the guitar pick down the strings. "You want another song?" I asked, smiling.

"Yes!" they shouted and clapped. Some whistled.

Wow. This kind of attention could go to my head fast. The response was insane.

I met Boone's eye, and he smiled at me, nodding in encouragement.

"Okay. This is a song I wrote about friendship and fun," I said, starting to strum at a lively pace.

Natalie cheered because she knew which one I was going to sing. It was a party song I wrote back when she and I were in college about being out with friends, and it fit the bar vibe perfectly.

Riley held her phone up, taking photos or filming me as I started in. By the time I finished, I had half the bar singing along with the chorus, Natalie leading them because she knew the song inside and out.

Everyone was on their feet. The crowd cheered, and I thanked them, waving, then walked off the stage.

Boone was there to take my guitar and wrap me up in a giant hug. "That was amazing, baby." The noise was loud, but I heard him over it. "Truly. You're next-level."

The adrenaline was buzzing, I felt so good. Still, I was always critical of myself. "Well, I messed up a few times–"

"You were perfect," he said firmly. "Nobody heard any mess ups. I know I didn't. And if they did, nobody cared because you were fucking *perfect*."

I lost my breath in his praise. Tears filled my eyes. Good tears. I wiped them away and smiled up at him.

Boone was so different from Marty. My ex used to point out all the things I could've done better. All the mistakes I made. He'd acted like he was my manager, and he was going to coach me into improving. I realized, suddenly, that we'd never been equals. Marty had seen himself as better than me. Older, wiser, smarter. He was going to "help" me with my career. But actually, all he'd done was crush all the spirit right out of me.

Boone was a partner. He might be a heck of a lot smarter than I was. He was definitely stronger. Faster. And superhuman. But he didn't act like he was better. He'd let me tie him up. Set rules for him. He wanted me to feel safe with him just as I wanted him to just be him without having to be cautious around me.

"Everybody here just fell madly in love with you," Boone said, kissing me full on the lips. "Including me, and I was already fucking head over heels."

If I'd been a light, I'd glow so bright you'd need sunglasses.

The Barn Cat members passed me to climb on the stage, congratulating me.

"That's going to be an impossible act to follow," one of them said. "Natalie, why didn't we open for *her*?"

I flushed with their praise, and Boone gave me a squeeze.

Our friends also showered me with compliments when I sat down as the Barn Cats took the stage. Ace raised his hand, and I gave him a high five. Roy winked.

This was what I'd missed being married. Marty had isolated me from my friends and family. I'd felt so alone. Now, I had community again. I had family.

But Boone had been self-isolating before we met. Even from his own brothers. He was punishing himself for his past. I knew from personal experience how horrible it was to not feel connected to people you loved. I wasn't going to let Boone isolate anymore.

"That was epic," Riley leaned over to say. "I'm posting the video on social media." She held up her phone screen to show me the video of me playing the last song. "Do you have an account I can tag?"

I shook my head. God, I'd lost touch completely with how to market myself. I didn't have the slightest clue where to begin, and I hadn't had energy to do anything besides getting divorce papers filed, coming to Cooper Valley, and earning enough money to get back on my feet.

"Let's start one up tonight," Boone suggested.

"What?" I laughed.

"Yeah, baby. Because you're going to be famous, and you'll need a way to reach your fans." He took my phone from my purse and held the screen up to my face to unlock it. "I'll get it set up for you."

As the Barn Cats started their first song, a lively tempo with Natalie playing the melody on the fiddle, my glow burned brighter. I felt so taken care of. So supported. Suddenly, everything felt possible. Even the actualization of the old dreams that I'd let fizzle out and die.

21

BOONE

FOR A WEEK, things were amazing. When Summer worked at Cody's, I picked her up, arriving a little early to help with cleanup. Then we spent the night at her place on Rand and Natalie's ranch. One night, I'd replaced the bed with one Roy had recently built. It was made of logs I'd cut down and hewn and sturdy enough to handle any kind of lovemaking.

When Summer had off, we stayed in my cabin on the mountain. I could've sat and stared at her all day. Hell, I could've kept her in bed, naked, and never let her out.

But I had trees to cut, and she had songs to write. I

loved knowing that after a hard day outside, I had her to come home to.

Her music. Her smiles. Her cries of pleasure when I always satisfied her.

She was less fearful, her wariness slipping away with each day that passed. I was proving through words and actions that I was trustworthy, that I only had her best interest at heart.

That while she was mine, I was hers, too.

On a bright, sunny day a week after her performance, I returned from Roy's woodshop to find Riley sitting with Summer at the kitchen table. They had mugs of hot cocoa in front of them.

They both looked up when I came in, stomping snow off my boots and taking off my jacket.

I sat on the bench by the door and tugged them off as I greeted Riley.

"This is a nice surprise," I said. "You two staying at Cody's place up here on the mountain?"

She nodded and smiled. "Yes, for two nights. Cody's taking a well-needed break."

Then she blushed, and there was no way either Summer or I could miss it. Their break definitely involved a lot of sex.

I stood in my sock-covered feet and went over to Summer, leaned down and kissed the top of her head, ready for a little sexy time of our own.

"Riley came to tell me my song went viral," Summer announced, beaming.

I looked to the younger woman, who looked beyond excited.

"Oh?"

Riley nodded and grinned then flipped her cell around to face me. "It's insane. I put up a clip right after the show last week. Then I added a few more. The first one, with that last fun song you played, has over a million views. And it's still climbing!"

I looked at Summer, hoping she had her friend's enthusiasm.

"I told you everyone would like it," I said.

Riley wasn't the only one who was crazy about Summer's music and helping her promote it. The morning after the concert, I'd reached out to Sara Mayes, a former client who was a record producer, with the links to Riley's original post. She was the one I'd mentioned to Summer, but I hadn't told her that I'd reached out. I was loving her excitement and newfound interest in songwriting and didn't want to curb any of that if Sara wasn't interested.

"People are using the clip of music for their own posts," Riley said, eyes on her phone. "I don't watch a ton of social media like some of my friends, but even I know this is nuts."

"I'm not sure what to–"

My cell rang from the pocket in my flannel. I pulled it out and saw that it was Sara calling. "Hey, Sara."

"Boone. Glad I got you. Wow, that woman you shared, she's on fire."

I looked to Summer, who was now chatting softly with Riley, their heads together as they looked at Riley's phone.

"Told you," I told Sara.

"I listened to it right away and loved it, but had to go to a shoot in Jamaica and just got back."

"Rough life," I muttered but softened it with a laugh.

"Thanks to you," she countered. "I circled back to the clip on the plane, and holy shit, it's taken off. How many calls has she gotten?"

"Calls?"

"From producers. I'm sure I've missed out."

"No. You haven't. She's open to hearing what you have to say, I'm sure."

Fuck, I was so proud of Summer. Her music was wanted for a talent she didn't seem to realize she had. It'd been shut down for so long, she doubted herself. Hopefully now, with Riley's help, she could see that it wasn't just a bar in Cooper Valley or a concert venue in Missoula where she was liked, but the world over.

"That's great."

But then I paused, thinking about what I'd done.

"Sara, you're not interested because you think you owe me one, do you?"

She laughed. "Boone. I do owe you one. More than one, but this? Her? No. I wouldn't give a music contract to someone who sucked. It's my butt on the line, too."

I sighed. "Okay. Right. You want to talk to her?"

"She's there?"

"She's my girl," I said.

Riley and Summer looked up at that.

"Wow, Boone. I'm happy for you. And yes, I want to talk to your soon-to-be-superstar girlfriend."

I passed the cell to Summer. "Someone wants to talk to you."

Summer took the phone with a frown. "Hello?"

Riley stood and came over. "Everything okay?"

"Oh yeah. It's a friend who–"

"WHAT?" Summer screeched then popped to her feet. "You want a demo? Yes, I can put that together. Totally. Oh my God!"

If I didn't know who was on the phone and what was being offered, I'd have panicked. Summer was upset and agitated and... shit, crying.

"Yes. I... yes. Oh my God! Yes! Right away!" I liked what she was saying to Sara, but I wanted her to say just that to me when I made her come next.

She hung up her call and turned to me. Stared up

at me, a tear sliding down her cheek, a smile on her face.

"What? What happened?" Riley asked.

Summer licked her lips and looked at Riley. "Your clip got seen by a producer. She wants a demo to decide whether to sign me. I might be getting a recording contract."

Riley hugged Summer and started jumping up and down. I grinned.

I didn't remember the last time I felt like this. I was so fucking happy because my girl was happy. Her dreams were my dreams, and I'd make them happen, any way I could.

22

SUMMER

I HUMMED to myself making us dinner while Boone showered. It was grilled cheese and soup I'd found in his freezer in a container labeled SOUP. As it thawed, I discovered it was beef vegetable and the tangy scent of it filled the cabin. Riley had left after I promised to keep her updated.

I might be getting a music contract.

Me.

I put the spatula up to my face like a microphone and sang a few lines before flipping the melty, buttery sandwiches.

I was happy. Insanely, over-the-top, happy.

A music contract.

A MUSIC CONTRACT. Wait. On our snowy walk last week, Boone had mentioned he knew someone in the business. Was this person, Sara, her? I'd been so excited and overwhelmed, I hadn't put it together until now.

I turned off the flame beneath the soup and grilled cheese sandwiches and went to the bathroom door. I could hear the water running. I knocked lightly then entered. The room was steamy and warm.

"Boone?"

He stuck his head out around the shower curtain. His hair was wet and soapy, sticking up in all directions. "Everything okay?"

"Yeah. I was thinking..." I dropped onto the closed lid of the toilet.

He slid the curtain back in place and probably started rinsing the shampoo from his hair.

"Who is this Sara person? I was too excited to remember her last name."

"Sara Mayes," he said.

The bathroom had white walls and quartz that covered the floor and halfway up the walls and a beautiful vanity. The clawfoot tub looked old, like he'd found it somewhere and installed it here for the space to look vintage. It worked. It blended in with the cabin style perfectly. A fluffy tan bathmat was beneath my toes.

"Right. You mentioned you knew her. So you reached out?"

The water shut off, and a second later, the tan and white striped shower curtain slid all the way back.

There was Boone. Naked. Wet. God, he was gorgeous.

He stepped onto the bathmat and grabbed a towel from the rack.

"Yes. She was a client of mine when I worked in New York. Thought she might be interested."

He ran the towel through his hair, drying it, but making it stick up every which way.

Once dry, he wrapped the towel around his waist.

Sitting, I was so much shorter.

"She's um, not just doing this because you're friends, is she?"

Of course, what did I care? A request for a demo was a request for a demo, even if my gorgeous lumberjack pulled strings for me. But I just wanted to know the deal.

He took my hand and tugged me out of the bathroom. I sat on the bed as he went to the dresser–which of course Roy probably made–and pulled out a pair of boxers. He shucked the towel and tugged them on, giving me a really nice view of his taut ass before it was covered in plaid cotton.

I forgot what I asked and perhaps even my name as I ogled.

"No. I even asked her that when she called. She said she wouldn't sign someone she couldn't get behind fully."

"How well do you know her?" I was still trying to figure out how he connected me with a *music producer*. It was incredible.

"Well..." A shadow passed over his face.

I remembered him saying he'd left his job because of some trouble. Was she part of that?

He turned, came over to the bed and sat beside me. The bed dipped so much I tipped against his side. His skin was warm and damp, even through my sweatshirt.

"I worked for a big hedge fund, handling rich people's money. She was one of my clients."

"But?"

He flashed a rueful smile. "You know me pretty well."

I reached for his hand, smiling back. "Getting there."

"She works for a big recording company out of New York. One time, she came to my office, and I could tell something was wrong. She was jittery and flustered. Maybe it was my amazing personality, but I got her to tell me what was bothering her."

"Amazing personality?" I smiled. "Go on."

"She said she had a stalker, and she thought she'd been followed on the way over. She thought it was a musician she'd turned down. He'd become obsessed with her. She said he was probably harmless, but I could tell she was scared shitless."

"That's awful."

"I said I'd walk her out and talk to the guy if we saw him." He shrugged. "I'm a big guy. I can be persuasive."

"Of course, you did." I hadn't known Boone that long, but everything about him suggested he was a gentleman, even with women he wasn't dating. No question he would offer to protect her.

He drew in a long breath and held it.

I turned, bending my knee so I faced him. "What?"

He nodded, looking down at his hands. His body was so big, muscles so thick they looked sculpted. The dark hair on his chest was soft. His skin was warm. He was big, but gentle. Fierce, but... God. Protective.

"I went outside with her, and we stood around out front while she waited for a cab. Sure enough, she spotted him leaning against a building across the street. We acted like we hadn't seen him and crossed over, pretending we were having a conversation. When we got close, he ducked into an alley.

"I chased. I'm fast. Way faster than a human."

My heart thudded against my chest at the story, even though it had happened years ago. It felt like something bad had transpired. Something Boone regretted. My heart preemptively hurt for him.

God, was this love?

Was I already in love with this man?

I was. Oh my God. I was.

"Then what?" I prompted when he stopped speaking. I was breathless.

"Well, I caught him."

Why did Boone look so miserable?

"He.. um, had a knife, and he stabbed me."

I squeezed his hand. "What?"

He shrugged. "It was a surface wound. But my wolf went berserk. You know, I was living in a big city. My wolf didn't get out to run enough. I told you about the full moon runs, but sometimes we need to run to let off steam. It makes us feel a hell of a lot better, but it's pretty much impossible to do in New York. I'd been living among humans thinking I was perfectly safe, but when I caught the guy, I lost control. It was the same as when I fought with my dad, only this guy wasn't a wolf."

I stared at Boone with big eyes, almost afraid to hear what was next. "Did you kill him?" I managed to ask.

Boone scrubbed a hand across his beard. "Almost. I could've. So easily. I was beating him up. Sara was screaming my name, trying to get me to stop." He shook his head. "Then–fuck, I could've hurt her–"

I waited, but Boone stopped telling the story. He looked straight ahead with an unfocused gaze, like he was reliving the moment.

"What happened?" I whispered.

He dropped his gaze to the floor then to me. Regret washed over his expression. "She forced herself between us." He shook his head. "That had been so fucking dangerous. But I guess my protective instincts took over the destructive ones, and I finally got control. He ended up in the hospital with all kinds of things broken."

I swallowed hard. "Were you arrested?"

He shook his head. "No. It was deemed self defense. Everyone celebrated it like I was some kind of fucking hero. Can you believe that? My boss loved it, but it didn't matter. I knew I was done in New York City."

I frowned. "What do you mean?"

"I mean, it was wrong. What happened. Me, losing control like that. I realized I was a danger to the humans around me. I hadn't spontaneously shifted, but I still had let my wolf lead. I'd shown my super-human strength. Plus, I had this stab wound that healed within days, and I had to pretend it hadn't. It was a clusterfuck, and I realized I needed to stay away from civilization."

"Does Sara know you're a shifter?"

He shook his head. "No. Like I said, I didn't shift. She just thought I was just crazy strong. And maybe just a little plain crazy."

"So you moved back here because of that?" Meaning up here on the mountain, isolated.

He nodded. "I almost beat another person to death."

He thought he was a danger to people. After what he did to his father and then to this other jerky guy.

"Oh, Boone." I took his hand. "You're not a danger to civilization. You knew when to pull back. When Sara got between you and her stalker, you stopped. You're a protector."

I realized then that Boone couldn't be any more opposite from Marty than I ever imagined. Boone had come on strong right from the first moment we met. He showed his power then and constantly after. Breaking the bed. Carrying me through the forest. Holding himself back over and over to make sure I was okay, that I could trust him.

Marty had been sweet and kind to start with. Charming. Wooed me with smiles and gifts and really good lies. Then, his true personality came out. Dark. Egotistical. Mean.

Boone had always shown me his true colors. Even when it was hard to admit things about himself. He never hid them. Not once did they waver, and he was amazing.

Marty hid them, and he was awful.

I was falling for Boone and started to love that I was his mate. He might have hurt that asshole in New York, but I knew I was safe with him.

He shook his head. "No. I can't control myself and my strength. I go wild. Feral. I'm dangerous."

I hopped to my feet, so I stood in front of him then climbed in his lap. His hands went to my hips as I set mine on his shoulders.

I waited until his dark eyes met mine. I saw hurt there. Guilt. Fear. Worry. He was afraid of hurting me which meant I was the only one who could relieve him of all those feelings. To let go and leave them behind. If I was starting new, then he could, too. "You did the right thing. You protected Sara when she needed it. You stood up to your dad when he was bullying you."

"I beat a man."

"Yeah, well, he stabbed you! And he might have stabbed Sara instead or worse. He deserved it."

Boone blinked but stayed quiet.

"He deserved it," I repeated. I cupped his cheeks with my hands. "*He deserved it.*"

His dark eyes searched mine for a minute, then his

shoulders dropped. His forehead rested against mine. "Baby, thank you."

"You don't have to put yourself in this self-imposed time out anymore, Boone," I told him.

His brows popped.

"You're carrying a lot of guilt around. What if it was time to just... put it down? Let it go? Come back to the land of the living?"

"Is that *land of the living* with you in it?" His voice cracked a little.

I nodded.

"Yeah?" The corner of his mouth tipped up.

I swallowed, nodding again. My heart beat against my chest in recognition of what he was asking. "I'm... I've fallen for you, Boone."

"Even... even knowing what I did?"

I nodded, then he grabbed my hips and turned, laying me down on the bed with him hovering over me. I smiled at how easily and gently he handled me.

"I love you, Summer."

I lost my breath as his lips descended, and he kissed me like he wanted to devour me.

23

BOONE

Summer arched her sweet body up to meet mine as I slammed my lips down over hers. I told myself to be gentle, but the message wasn't getting through from my brain to my body. The need to claim her had me feverish, but it was more than biology. She seemed to like it. Craved the contact as much as me.

It was love. That very human emotion I had somehow avoided until now.

She was my mate, but I was also madly in love.

Summer saw me. Like, truly saw me. Not for who she thought I was supposed to be or should be but for who I truly was. She saw and knew my failings and still wanted to be with me. Saw my wounds and wanted to help me heal them.

She wasn't afraid of me. Summer, the woman who had an asshole ex.

"Baby, I need you," I found myself saying moments before I ripped her sweatshirt in half.

I tried to check my strength, calm my aggression, but the scent of Summer's arousal filled the room, and I was lost.

Thank fuck I was only in my boxers.

"You have me," she murmured, helping me by unhooking her bra. Thank fuck for front clasps, too.

I unzipped her jeans and dragged them off her hips right along with her panties.

"Oh, *damn*." Her laugh was breathy.

"I need to be inside you. Fucking you. Making you come." I'd lost all ability to reason. The raw words just tumbled from my lips.

"I need that, too." She spread her knees wide for me.

I growled, kissing down her body. "Thank fuck."

My cock throbbed, tenting my boxers. I lowered my head between her legs to feast there, sucking and licking her with so much passion I lost all nuance.

She didn't seem to care. Her hips bucked and writhed, and her cries grew more desperate.

I started to slide a finger inside her, but she tugged

on my hair. I looked up at her bare body to meet her blue eyes. She shook her head.

"No. I want your cock. I want you inside me."

Oh, damn. She didn't have to tell me twice, and what my girl wanted, my girl got.

I rose and shucked my boxers.

The room spun. Heat came off me in waves. I knew my eyes had to be glowing pale green, showing my wolf.

Summer didn't look scared, though. She looked as delirious as I felt.

I climbed back on the bed and lifted one of her knees toward her body to give me full access. Her pussy was slick, pink, and smelled so fucking good.

"You want this cock?" I growled, rubbing the head over her swollen slit.

"Yes," she moaned, lifting her hips.

Before I could even think to modulate my strength, I speared her with my erection.

She gasped, her body shooting up on the bed before I snapped my hand out to catch her throat. I didn't know I was into hand necklaces, but I sure as fuck was now.

"Beautiful girl," I murmured, forcing myself to slow my arcs in and out of her. "My incredible, talented, kind-hearted, beautiful mate."

She smiled before her mouth opened wide, and her head fell back as I shoved in deeper.

"Boone," she moaned. Her internal muscles squeezed around my cock like a tight glove.

"Oh, fuck," I muttered.

She gave another squeeze, and my control slipped away.

"Fuck, baby." I pounded into her harder. The room began to spin around us. "Fuck, fuck."

She tightened her muscles again, urging me on.

"Fate. You feel so good, I can't...I...Summer–" I lost the thread of reason. I needed to mark my mate. To make her mine.

Nothing else made sense to me.

"Are you going to mark me?" Summer panted.

I blinked several times, hard. Sweat dripped from my forehead. Our bodies undulated together in a pool of slick.

"What?"

Did I hear that right? Or was my wolf playing tricks on me?

Did she *ask* me to mark her?

Or had I turned feral?

Summer didn't know about claiming. I hadn't explained the mating bite to her yet because she'd been so skittish, especially about the notion of belonging to me. Understandable after what she'd been through. Yet she'd known about me being a shifter. I hadn't had to tell her about that.

She must've seen my confusion because she explained, "Natalie told me."

Thank fuck. I was actually relieved that she knew, especially right now when I was balls deep inside her. I'd have to remember to get a list of everything she learned from her friend. Fill in any blanks because there would be nothing between us.

"I need…" I couldn't formulate other words to finish the sentence. My dick didn't care because my body was on autopilot–plowing into Summer like it was my ticket to heaven. "I need…I need…" Desperation crept in. What if I made another mistake? What if my wolf had taken over again, or I'd gone feral? What if she didn't want this?

"Stop thinking, baby," she said. "Do it."

"Summer!" I shouted, either giving her one last chance to change her mind or telling her in some way that I wasn't sure I could hold off a second longer.

"Mark me, Boone!" she cried.

Panic spiked through me. I couldn't–I was going to hurt her. My wolf was dangerous. He might–

It didn't matter what I thought because my fangs had already elongated, ready to permanently embed my scent into her skin.

"Sss…" I tried to speak, to say her name. I wanted to

reason with Summer. With myself. I wanted to slow things down, but I couldn't.

"I mean it," she said. "Do it."

It was too late. My balls contracted. Cum shot down my shaft. My vision went black, and then I tasted blood as I bit her shoulder.

Summer!

She convulsed beneath me, crying out.

Wait...no. Moaning?

Summer's internal muscles fluttered around my cock, milking it for my release. She was orgasming. Holy shit, she was coming and crying out my name. Writhing beneath me in pleasure. Milking my dick, so it'd fill her pussy with more of my cum.

I carefully, gently, extracted my fangs from her trapezius muscle as I stroked in and out of her with slow glides. She was so full of cum it seeped out, coated us. The bed.

"Baby," I croaked. I licked the blood away, using my saliva to speed the healing process. "Fuck, baby. Please say you're okay?"

I lifted my head to see her gorgeous face better.

"I'm okay," Summer panted, a post-sex smile on her face, like she was drunk and happy.

"You are? Fuck, I didn't plan on marking you tonight. I know you had problems with me laying claim to you, and I respect that and–"

Summer put her fingers to my lips. "I'm okay. I wanted it. Like I said, Natalie explained it all to me."

My throat closed with emotion. Thank fuck. She was okay. I didn't hurt her. At least not too badly.

"What...what did she explain?"

"That you belong to me now." Summer lifted her chin. Raising her hand, she brushed my damp hair back. Her stroke was soft, and I knew it'd feel just like that when she petted my wolf for the first time.

I stared at her. *She* was claiming *me?* Relief and celebration swept from my heart to my limbs. I couldn't help but laugh.

"I sure as fuck do, baby. I belong to you. Every breath I take will be for you."

Her eyes filled with tears, and concern slammed back into me. I frowned, my gaze roving over her.

"Is it starting to hurt? Did I fuck you too rough?"

"No." She gave a watery laugh. "I'm happy, and I like it rough."

My dick stirred inside her because I liked rough, too. Or at least like what we just did. Just as I was learning what made her happy, I was learning what made me happy.

"Fuck, baby. I'm so happy. My wolf is happy." I eased out of her, my gaze roving over her face, memorizing every perfect detail. "You're mine," I breathed.

This time, instead of flinching or freaking out, she

nodded, her palm sliding down to cradle the side of my face. I turned my head and kissed it. "I'm yours. You're mine. This is our beginning."

This was our beginning. I couldn't believe it. It was almost too good to be true.

But my wolf had settled. I was fully bonded to my mate—attached and protective and needing to provide, but that feral desperation was gone. I wasn't going to go moon mad.

"But I think our dinner has gone cold," she said.

I chuckled. "Fuck dinner. I'm feasting on you."

And I did just that. More than once.

24

SUMMER

I WAS HAPPY. I couldn't really remember ever being this happy. I had friends. Natalie, of course, but the entire Wolf Ranch group had taken me in. It wasn't because they were all shifters either because they weren't. Audrey and Marina were sisters and human. Charlie and Becky and Riley and… I could keep going, but the names didn't matter. They were all my newfound friends.

"Another pitcher, please and thank you," a guy in a snap shirt and Stetson requested with a wink. It was Saturday night again–time moved fast when your days and nights were filled with sex and love and belonging. Even though it was snowing out, the place was packed.

A little weather didn't bother Montanans much. If it did, they'd be stuck in their houses for eight months out of the year.

I reached to the middle of the high top and grabbed the empty pitcher. "You got it."

I weaved through the crowd, saying hi to some familiar faces and set the empty on the server area of the bar. Cody came over.

"Refill, please."

He nodded, tucked the pitcher in the dirties bucket, and started filling a clean one. As he did, he glanced my way. "All good?"

I smiled, which I knew he couldn't miss. "Yeah. Really good."

He tapped his neck, right where I'd been marked on mine. "Figured."

After Boone had marked me, I'd looked at the spot in the mirror. It wasn't too sore or even much of an open wound where his teeth punctured the skin. Now, it was just red marks where he'd done it. A small scar. It didn't look like a hickey, so humans who didn't know about shifters wouldn't think it was anything. But Cody recognized it for what it was.

Boone was mine.

"Where's your mate tonight?" He flipped off the tap.

"With his brothers," I replied over the new song on

the jukebox. It was loud and twangy and had a solid beat that everyone liked. "They were going snowmobiling with Johnny and Rand earlier. Then some kind of guy thing. Sports on TV or whatever. He's coming before closing to pick me up."

And take me back to my place and hopefully have his snarly way with me.

This was a new thing for Boone–doing something fun with his brothers and other shifters–but a good transition because it was up on the mountainside where he felt the most comfortable. He was working on *getting out there,* and I was proud of him for it.

"That's great. Maybe you two can come over for dinner some night I have off. Riley's been super excited telling me about how your songs have gone viral online."

I'd heard from the music producer again, wanting to hear an official demo reel and meet me.

I felt myself blush and rolled my eyes. "Yeah, she's my social media manager, for sure."

"You're good, Summer. She might've put it out there, but people love your work." He set the full pitcher in front of me.

I smiled again, this time not because of Boone but because of me. He was giving me a compliment, and I liked it. Sure, everyone liked compliments, but my music had been shut down for so long it was validating to know people like Cody really liked it. Millions of views were also proof.

"Sounds good."

"Great." He rapped his knuckles on the bar. "After you deliver that, can you grab some clean bar rags from the storeroom? We're running low."

"Sure, no problem."

I headed off, pitcher in hand, humming my latest song I'd thought up when Boone and I had been walking in the woods. The melody was coming together–at least in my head–even with the loud music inside the bar. After dropping it off, I veered toward the back. In the storage room, I flipped on the light and found the bin with the clean bar rags.

The door slammed shut, and I spun around, startled. A gasp replaced my humming.

There stood Marty. Military buzz cut. Close shave. Tanned skin. Ice blue eyes. Blond hair. Short, stocky physique.

My heart pounded, and my skin tingled from the surge of adrenaline at seeing him after all these months.

"Hello, Summer." His voice was as I remembered. Deep. Even. Taunting. "Miss your husband?"

My initial reaction was panic. He'd conditioned me to placate him when he was in this mood. By the end, I feared him. But then I remembered where I was. Who

I was now. I didn't care about keeping him calm. I didn't care what he thought about me. I wasn't going to let him push me around anymore.

"What are you doing here?" I poured as much anger into my question as I could muster.

His eyes narrowed. My heart pounded, recognizing danger. "I can't stop in and see my wife?"

I didn't like the way he kept reminding me that we were still married. "No. We're not together anymore."

He slowly shook his head. "You've had your little fun. It's time to come back."

This man was absolutely delusional. "Not happening. We're getting divorced."

"Only if I sign the papers, which I'm not."

I ground my teeth. "I will still get the divorce, even if you contest it. You need to leave. I don't want to be with you. I don't even like you."

He shrugged. "You've always been so dramatic, Summer. Flighty. Look at you, working in a bar. You can barely take care of yourself."

"I'm doing just fine," I said, way more angry than scared now. How dare he show up here! I'd gotten past getting bullied and pushed around. Past contorting myself for an asshole in order to keep the peace. Past *him.*

"Living in a small town in Montana? Working as a

barmaid where men are leering at you? I saw the way that guy winked. At *my* wife."

"I don't know which guy you're talking about–"

"Exactly. You've been flirting with men all night."

"Not. Your. Business, Marty. We're not together. I can flirt with whomever I want."

"So you're whoring yourself out?" His jaw clenched. I recognized that look. He was getting pissed. That meant danger.

I could have Cody throw him out if I could get past him "You need to leave, Marty. We're done. I've got a new life now. I'm singing, and I have a–"

"Yeah, you're singing. I saw the video online. What the fuck were you wearing? Have you seen the comments guys have left? They're all for your tits. Not your song. Thousands and thousands want to fuck *my wife*."

"I'm not your wife!" I snapped.

He took a step closer. We were in the storeroom. Door closed. But I wasn't alone. Back in Los Angeles, he'd isolated me from my friends to make me fully dependent on him. Here, I had an entire community that would kick his ass if he touched me, starting with Boone.

"You are. Legally."

"Not for long."

"We're not getting divorced. You're mine. You want

to whore yourself out by making money with your music, that's fine, but that money's mine."

Oh my God. He'd probably seen the video clip. Maybe not him because he didn't watch music videos, but maybe someone at the station had. He'd seen how successful I was, how people were responding. *That* was how he'd found me. He'd been putting me down for years, and *now* he wanted in on it? He wanted the money. The fucking money.

"You said I wasn't good enough yet. I guess you were wrong about me."

He stepped, so he was right in front of me. I didn't back down but tipped my chin back, so I could meet his gaze. He wasn't anywhere near the size of Boone. In fact, he looked downright scrawny in comparison. But he was still a few inches taller than me, and I knew how nasty he was.

"You're going to get your whore ass in the car, and we're getting the hell out of this podunk town."

"I'm not going anywhere with you." I was proud that my voice didn't quaver.

"You are," he snapped.

I ducked and weaved to get around him, but he grabbed my hair and tugged me back.

I cried out at the pain in my scalp, whirling to shove him.

Then he backhanded me, the sound echoing off

the walls of the small room. I put my hand to my cheek. His wedding ring had cut my cheek, and I dabbed at the trickling blood. When I turned my head back to look him in the eye, I saw the gun.

It was his service pistol. He wasn't on duty. He wasn't even in the same state as where he was a police officer.

"Let's go, Summer," he snapped. In all the time we'd been married, I'd never seen him like this before. "I've had enough of you acting out. Make a scene, and I'll shoot someone. It'll be your fault."

I was reeling from his presence. From what he had planned. From the strike. My brain ran through quick calculations. I knew from Boone's story that Cody could take a bullet and survive, but I didn't know how many patrons out there were shifters. Maybe none. If he shot them or me, we'd die.

Even if Cody could hear me scream over the music, I couldn't risk signaling for help. Not with Marty in this kind of mood with his weapon drawn.

He grabbed my wrist and threw open the storeroom door, tugged me down the hall to the back emergency exit. I slapped my hand on the wall to keep from falling before we went out into the back of the parking lot. And a snowstorm.

25

BOONE

I HAD fun with Ace and Roy and the guys from Wolf Ranch. I hadn't been on a snowmobile in years. But I could only go so long with hanging with them before I told them I had to get to my mate.

Fortunately, they didn't say anything other than giving me a wave or a slap on the back before I headed down the mountain.

I'd thought since I'd claimed Summer that my need for her would lessen. That now that she carried my mark, my scent embedded in her, my dick wouldn't guide my every action. I'd be sane.

I was so fucking wrong. My dick wanted me to get to Summer now. To grab her hand and lead her back into the storeroom and fuck her. Last time, I'd only eaten her pussy in that small space. This time, I'd bend her over and take her from behind and–

"Fuck," I groaned and drove faster. Or at least as fast as I could go with the snow falling the way it was.

I was thankful that she'd agreed to have Cody pick her up from her little apartment at Rand and Natalie's on his way into the bar instead of her driving in this. I needed to get her that better car. A raised SUV with a shit ton of weight. Four-wheel drive. All the safety bells and whistles.

Until then, I'd happily be her chauffeur.

When I entered Cody's, I went to the bar and greeted my friend. Glanced around. "Busy night." I unzipped my coat and looked for Summer.

"Sure is." Cody reached across the bar to shake my hand. "Happy for you."

He knew I'd claimed Summer. Any shifter wouldn't be able to miss it.

"Thanks." I scanned the room. "Where's Summer?"

He grabbed two empty glasses. "She was getting some rags for me from the storeroom."

The storeroom. Fuck, yes. My dick got hard just thinking about taking her in there as I wanted.

"I'll go help her."

He grinned. "Right. I guess take your time but don't mess shit up in there."

I smiled back, rubbed my hands together. "No problem."

People moved out of my way as I cut through the bar and toward the back hallway. The storeroom door was open, and I strode inside.

It was empty; the box of rags on the floor was tipped over. I couldn't miss my mate's scent. It was strong in the room, but I picked up another scent. Human. Male. But this was a bar, and there were a lot of humans here. I spun around. Walked into the hall.

I sniffed again, thinking I'd follow Summer's scent to the women's room, but instead, her scent went the other way, mingled with the same human's scent. It was stronger here–there was less confusion for my nose with others' scents because not many came this far back. The only thing down this way was the emergency exit.

I stared at the door then back at the storeroom.

My mate went from the storeroom out the back door with a human male?

The hairs on the back of my neck stood up. Something was wrong. My wolf growled. Then my eye caught on something on the wall.

There was wood wainscotting that came a few feet up the wall, but above that, the walls were painted white. A few framed photos were spread out depicting historical images of Cooper Valley.

I didn't notice them. I noticed the smear of blood. I leaned in and sniffed it.

Summer.

Fuck! My mate.

My mate's blood.

A genuine wolf-growl ripped from my throat. Someone once compared me to the Avenger who turned into a huge green monster-like version of himself when he got angry. That was me now. I almost spontaneously shifted.

Summer was in trouble. I threw open the emergency door, breaking one of the hinges. Out into the parking lot I scanned for my mate. She was nowhere to be seen. Her scent wasn't in the air. It was snowing, and the wind was blowing. Footprints were there, but filling in quickly.

He took her. It had to be her asshole ex. Summer hadn't mentioned he was in town or coming to town or him even contacting her. Which means she hadn't expected him. He hurt her, and he took her out of here forcefully.

I was going to tear his arms and legs from his body.

I ran the path. Two sets of footprints. They led to an empty parking spot. Tire tracks were visible. The vehicle had backed out to the right, then went left... toward the lot's exit onto Main Street.

He had my mate. She was bleeding. There was no

way in hell she'd have gone off with someone without telling at least Cody. And she wouldn't have been able to go with someone unwillingly through the main bar.

My fists clenched. My wolf pushed to the front. I couldn't scent her any longer.

Ever since the first time I picked up her scent here at the bar, I'd held myself in check. I was cautious. Afraid I'd hurt her or scare her away. I walked gently. Talked softly. Fucked carefully, even when she said she liked it rough.

Now? Fuck all that. I was done being careful and safe and cautious. I was tired of pretending I could be any of those things because the real me, the vicious, ruthless, dangerous me was coming out.

I tipped my head back and roared into the night.

26

SUMMER

"Take me back, Marty," I said from the passenger seat of a small car. It was definitely a rental because it was spotlessly clean and had the brand-new car scent. Marty wouldn't be caught dead in this basic car in LA.

I shivered, my hands tucked between my thighs. My cheek throbbed from where he hit me. I only briefly entertained the thought of opening the door and throwing myself out of the moving vehicle, but even if I survived the impact, nothing would stop Marty from stopping and shooting me.

If I stayed put, I doubt he'd kill me since he seemed intent on taking me back to LA, but I wouldn't put him above shooting my kneecap to keep me from running then blame it on me for making him do it.

"Take you back to Cooper Valley?" he replied. "Fuck no. That town is filled with nothing but losers and hicks."

His hands gripped the wheel, and he was trying to handle the car in the bad weather. Even though he was a cop, there was no snow in southern California, and he had no idea what he was doing. After he slid the first time, I put on my seatbelt.

"You don't like me," I countered. "You thought I cheated. That I dressed sluttily. That I was a bad singer. Everything I did was bad. I did you a favor leaving you."

"Favor? Do you have any idea what people at work think? I can't show my face."

"People get divorced all the time!"

"I don't. *You* don't."

"I do. I don't want to be with you. I don't love you. Hell, I don't even like you."

His nasty gaze whipped to mine, and he seethed. "You are my wife. You are mine."

You are mine. Boone had said those exact words to me multiple times. I'd gotten upset at first for just this reason. Because Marty was crazy, and when he said it, he meant it in a non-consensual, kidnappy way.

With his eyes off the road and on me for even three

seconds, when he looked back, he'd missed the oncoming car. He overcorrected and slid toward the embankment. We spun once, doing a full circle like a ride at an amusement park. We'd missed the other car; it was long gone. They knew how to drive in snow.

My heart was in my throat, my hand on the dash. Marty slammed his hand on the steering wheel. "Jesus, fuck! What is this shitty weather? Who can live in an icebox like this? We've got to find a place to stay for the night."

I didn't say a word, but I was relieved. He was going to kill us if he kept going.

"I saw a motel by the highway," he said although I wasn't sure he was telling me or talking to himself. "It can't be much farther."

A motel with Marty. I couldn't jump out into the snowbank to escape him. There was nothing out here. Even though I couldn't see it through the darkness and the snow, only vast prairie was on either side of the two-lane road. I had no coat. No boots or hat. I still had my bar apron around my waist. I'd be dead in thirty minutes.

A motel, though, meant I was stuck in a room with Marty. With a bed. And his gun.

All I could do was hold out hope that someone discovered I was missing. Cody was expecting me to come back with bar rags. Hell, he was expecting me to do my job. Once he couldn't find me, he'd get concerned.

Boone was coming to pick me up. It was the first time I'd felt thankful my little car was crappy in snow, just like this rental. Boone would show up to collect me around last call and lose his shit when he couldn't find me in the bar.

He'd look for me. He'd come after me. He'd find me.

He had to.

27

BOONE

I STORMED AROUND THE BUILDING, following the tire tracks in the snow that merged into all the others from vehicles that had come and gone from the bar. There was no way to track her, not even in wolf form. I didn't have her scent nor know which way she'd been taken.

I entered the front door. I needed Cody's help. I had enough of a clear head to know that I shouldn't rage like a bull inside the bar, so I stood just inside of the entrance and called Cody's name. I yelled it, but it didn't even turn many heads because the place was so loud and packed. But Cody had impressive hearing, and my shout would be a surprise.

He looked immediately up from the pint glass he

was filling from the tap. He must've recognized something was wrong because he sat the glass down, called to the other bartender to take over and came over to me.

He pushed me back outside, and when the bar noise was muffled by the closed door and we stood alone in the snow, he asked, "What's the matter?"

"Summer's gone," I growled. "She's been taken." I raised my hands to my hair, tugged.

His eyes widened. "What the fuck? She went to get rags."

Rage made it hard for me to put sentences together. I was barely staying in human form. "Her blood..." I pointed toward the back exit. "He took her."

"Blood?" Cody's expression turns from concerned to grim. "Fuck! Who? Her ex?"

"Who else?"

"I don't know. She went viral this week. Could be any psychopath. C'mon. I've got security cameras. We'll see who took her and what kind of car they're driving." He hastily turned to go inside.

I tried to speak, but the only sound that came from my mouth was a deranged growl.

Cody stopped and turned. Pointed around the side of the building. "Go in the back door," he said. "You're not stable enough to handle all those people."

He was right, and thank fuck for that. I wasn't thinking straight.

Thirty seconds later, he opened the back door, where he stared at the broken hinge. "Did you do this?"

I growled and pointed out the blood on the wall.

"I see it." We both sniffed the air. Summer's scent was still here, but it was fading fast. "She was with a human male."

I lifted my face to the ceiling and let out a howl.

Cody clapped his hand over my mouth, smothering the eerie sound. "Not here, Boone. Come into my office." He led me right to his messy space. He pulled out his cell and made a call. "Levi. It's Cody. Get your ass over here. Someone's taken Boone's mate. Yeah, I'll have the footage pulled up by the time you get here. Come through the backdoor. Boone broke it, so it doesn't lock."

He dropped his cell on his desk then his butt in his office chair. Waking up his computer, he got to work as I prowled his small space.

"We'll find her," he promised. He looked away from the security footage he'd pulled up for a moment to meet my eyes. "We will. You've got an entire pack to help."

The video feed appeared on his screen, and my gaze shot to it. He had cameras set up on the front and back doors, and two aimed at the parking lot, for full coverage. He opened the feed from the back door and rewound through the last thirty minutes.

"There!" At least that's what I tried to say, but instead it came out as a roar. Cody stopped rewinding.

Oh fuck. There was Summer, being dragged by the arm by some skinny asshole. It was her ex. I knew because I'd already stalked him. With the little information Summer had shared, his name, and that he was a cop, and what I knew of her, I'd collected some data on the fucker. I'd already memorized his face in case he ever showed up here.

I picked up the metal garbage can beside his desk and crushed it into a ball.

Cody gave it a quick glance. "Okay, yeah. I didn't need that. Look, Boone, we've got his face. Let's get his vehicle." He opened the feed from one of the parking lot cameras and rewound thirty minutes.

Nothing.

I jabbed my finger at the icon of the feed from the other camera.

"Yeah. I'm on it." Cody clicked it open and rewound. "There they are."

I watched the asshole stuff Summer into the front seat of a blue Chevrolet Spark and take off in the direction of Missoula.

"They won't make it far in this snowstorm in that

car," Cody muttered. "Especially over the pass. Levi can put out an APB—"

I'd already torn off my clothes and shifted. I was gonna chase down that car and kill the man who touched my mate.

"Hang on–you'll be no help in wolf–"

I didn't wait to hear what Cody had to say–I was already racing through the snow at top wolf speed. A normal wolf could run up to forty-five miles per hour. A shifter's top speed was even faster.

Right now because of the storm, I ran at twice the speed of the cars on the highway. I could overtake that fucking Chevy Spark. I raced along the side of the highway, allowing my wolf instinct to lead.

Hang on, baby. I'm coming for you.

28

SUMMER

MARTY HANDCUFFED me to the steering wheel while he checked in at the motel. It was old, log cabin themed and had only one floor, the room entrances directly off the parking lot. I seethed, searching the dash for any kind of emergency notification system I could use to signal for help, but there was nothing. It was just a simple, cheap rental car.

"Let's go." He returned, opening my door and leaning across to unlock the handcuffs.

"What exactly is your plan here?" I demanded. "This doesn't make sense, Marty."

"Shut up, Summer." He fumbled with the lock

because the position was awkward. I kept talking while eyeballing his gun. It was back in the holster. The moment he released my hands, I was going to reach for it.

I would shoot the fucker, too.

He was unhinged. I couldn't believe I used to care about this man. Believed he'd cared about me. He wasn't capable of caring about anyone but himself.

"You can't keep me prisoner forever. How do you imagine that's going to work for you? I'm going to somehow make you money with my music but keep it a secret that I'm locked up in your house with you?"

He finally unlocked the cuffs but kept an iron grip on my closest hand, refastening the handcuff around my wrist.

Fuck. It was now or never. I kept talking, hoping to distract him.

"How do you think the guys at the station will take that? Although I guess they look the other way over a little domestic abuse, right?"

"I said, *shut up!*" Marty snarled.

He reached for my other wrist, so I took my chance, snatching at his gun with the wrist already attached to the cuffs.

I got it out of the holster, but his fist slammed into my face.

Pain exploded in my cheek, and my vision went black.

When I came back to consciousness, I was over Marty's shoulder as he slipped and slid across the snowy sidewalk and unlocked the door to the motel. My wrists were locked together in front of me, and his gun wasn't in the holster.

Dammit.

Marty stepped inside the motel room and threw me on the bed. "Don't move," he snarled as he shut the door, closing the cheap curtains, and drawing the security chain across. He kicked off his snowy boots.

My face throbbed so hard where he'd hit me I could feel my heart beating in my cheek. I brought my fingers to touch the area. It had already swelled.

Marty was out of his mind. He'd fully lost it.

When I was badgering him earlier, I'd realized the truth. As soon as he understood he couldn't win this, and there was no way it would ever work–that there was no way I'd ever go home and be his wife again–he'd end it. And I didn't mean he'd end it by letting me go. I meant he'd end *me*. Maybe end both of us in one of those stupid dramatic murder-suicide things that deranged men do.

It was that old twisted "If I can't have her, no one can" mentality.

So, I needed to get the fuck out of his clutches now

before he figured it out. Either that, or I needed to make him believe I would go home with him and be a good little wife until I could get away. But it was probably too late for that. I'd antagonized him too much now.

I closed my eyes and steadying my breath, trying to think through the pain.

I needed to get word to Boone. Tell him where I was.

Okay.

So I'd wait for a chance to use the phone. He had to go to the bathroom or–

"Are you hungry?" I tried to make my voice sound casual, like we were still husband and wife, figuring out what we were going to have for dinner.

"What? No!" he snapped. He paced back and forth, stabbing his fingers through his hair, which was now damp from melted snow.

I used my feet to scoot myself backward on the bed. It was awkward as hell with my hands cuffed together, but when my head hit the headboard, I rolled to my side and pushed with my feet until I could sit up, leaning against it.

"Did they have a vending machine in the lobby?" I asked.

Marty was a junk food fiend. I could plant the seed

that he'd go for snacks, and then I'd be able to make a call.

Marty ignored me, continuing to pace.

I kept my mouth shut and gave it some time. I'd been married to him for years. If I pushed too hard, it would be too obvious. I'd mentioned food and eventually, his stomach and junk food addiction would kick in, and he'd go back to the lobby. Then I could call 911 from the hotel phone.

I forced my breath to calm. The shock and pain in my cheekbone to subside. Forced myself to be patient.

Marty dropped onto the end of the other bed, clicked on the television and flipped through the channels. He stopped on one of the *Mission Impossible* movies.

When it cut to a commercial for Snickers, I knew the TV was doing the work for me.

Marty turned the volume up to the loudest the TV went. "I'll go buy some snacks." He walked to the nightstand and ripped the phone out from the wall.

Fuck!

He used the cord to tie my legs together then yanked my body off the bed. I fell to the floor with a thud. "I'm sure you thought you'd be running off while I'm getting food."

"No, I'm just hungry." I pretended to sulk.

He unlocked the handcuffs and looped them around the leg of the bed, then reattached them.

I definitely wasn't going anywhere, and unless his cell phone miraculously fell out of his pocket near my hands, I wasn't making any phone calls.

Dammit!

Marty clomped out, and I fought back tears. I was alone in a motel room with my dangerous ex. No one knew where I was.

Keep it together, Summer. Think. Think!

I couldn't lie here and play victim. I needed to have a plan for when he came back.

I tried to lift the bed to get my cuffs out, but it was hella heavy. I folded my body in half to get my fingers to the cord around my ankles.

Yes! That might work. I could reach the cord. I rolled to my side on the musty carpet and pulled my knees up to my chest to work on it. He'd wrapped it around my ankles a bunch of times and then tied a knot. My fingers shook as I loosened the ends to get it free.

Yes!

I yanked at the cord, which only tightened it, then forced myself to slow down and unwind it. My heart pounded, and my fingers shook. When it was free, I plugged the end into the phone jack near my head.

Now if I could only reach the phone he'd thrown across the room. Maybe with my feet?

I lengthened my body back out and tried to nudge the phone with my toe. I could just touch it...

The door swung open, and Marty walked in with a few snack bags and a can of soda. His face contorted with rage when he saw what I'd done.

"What in the fuck do you think you're doing?"

29

BOONE

I CAUGHT sight of the car in one of the motel parking lots along the frontage road of the highway. I raced toward it. My human brain knew I shouldn't let my wolf be seen in civilization, but my wolf wanted blood.

I didn't give a fuck about pack rules right now. I wanted blood, too.

I raced up to the car then slowed to catch the scent. The snow had muted everything, though. It was still falling, and the car was already covered with at least an inch of it. I'd prowl past every door to get Summer's scent. If not, I'd break into every fucking motel room until I found her.

I growled, scanning the motel doors. Most people parked in front of their room. I hoped this loser did that as well, especially since he was a fucking southern California asshole and couldn't handle a little winter weather.

Before I could do anything, Fate had my back.

I saw a guy stepping into one of the motel rooms. Skinny. Slick blond hair. Douchebag vibes. Marty. LAPD asshole. I knew him from my research on the bastard and recognized him from the security films from Cody's.

He was a dead man.

Dead.

I surged across the parking lot and threw myself at the door. It didn't fall in, but I didn't shift into human form. Fuck the door. I backed up and leapt at the window, smashing it in.

I tucked and rolled, coming up into a shitty little hotel room. Tan walls, weird orange light fixtures and matching carpet, now littered with broken glass.

Summer screamed from where she lay on the floor.

Marty twisted to look from where he was standing over her, fist cocked.

No, he fucking didn't. *He hit my mate?*

He. Hit. My. Mate.

I went blind with rage. Snarled.

Marty's eyes widened, stunned, then switched to fear.

I leaped across the room, my front paws knocking Marty away from Summer. He fell to the floor with a hard thud, and my teeth sank into the front of his throat. With a powerful snap of my head, I ended him.

I tasted his gore, his blood on my tongue. I whipped my head around to look at Summer, who kept screaming.

I snarled, rotating to see where other danger was. Who was making my mate scream?

"Boone!" That was Levi's voice. I looked up. He stood in the doorway, the door broken behind him. The curtains billowed around the broken window, and snow blew in.

Levi was here. He wore his sheriff uniform, but I could see the color change in his eyes. His wolf was showing, but not as much as mine.

He wouldn't hurt Summer.

I snarled again, my hackles raised, the taste of Marty's blood fouling my mouth. I lunged at the fucker again, biting his side and ripping to make sure he was dead.

"Boone, shift back!" Levi used alpha command on me. His human deputy, Kyle Abbott stood beside him.

His order didn't work because I was way more

fucking alpha than he was, but it made me pay attention.

I turned my bloody maw in his direction, then looked back at my mate.

Her face was swollen and bruised, eyes wide with terror. Marty'd had her on the floor, handcuffed to the fucking bed frame. She was hyperventilating, her chest rising and falling with rapid panting.

Seeing her like that further enraged me, and I snarled at Marty's body again. I would dismember him. I shouldn't have killed him so quickly. I should have made him suffer.

"Boone, you're scaring Summer." Levi put alpha command in his voice again. His hands were out, gun tucked away.

Scaring...Summer?

I looked to her. Saw the fear.

Oh no. My sweet mate. I'd scared her?

It was the one thing I tried never to do. Oh, shit.

Instantly, I shifted into human form and tried to assimilate what had happened from a two-legged perspective.

Fuck! I'd let her lie helpless on the ground while a wild beast ripped apart her ex. My first instinct should have been to free her. To hold her. To get her to safety. Instead, I'd gone feral and ruthlessly murdered someone in front of her. Not just severely injured like my father and the stalker in New York. Killed.

I murdered her ex.

"Summer," I croaked, wiping my mouth with the back of my hand.

She still looked afraid, even with me in human form. Of course, I was covered in her ex-husband's blood. I'd just killed a man in front of her. And she'd never even seen my wolf before. Had she even understood it was me?

I rushed forward to lift the bed up, so she wasn't pinned there. The second she was free, she rolled away. I lowered the bed and lifted her to her feet.

"Here." Abbott had fished the keys to the handcuffs out of Marty's pocket, and he tossed them to me.

It occurred to me that he didn't seem fazed by the fact that I was a wolf. But then, his daughter, Riley, was mated to Cody, so maybe he knew about our kind.

I quickly unlocked Summer's handcuffs and reached out to rub her raw wrists. I wanted to hold her, but she kept back, away from me. Her body trembled, and even over the stench of Marty's blood, I could smell her fear.

My mate was afraid. Of me.

As she should be. I was fucking dangerous. Just as I always knew.

Fate, I'd just done it again! I'd lost control and

taken things way too far. My wolf was a liability. I was a danger to my own beautiful mate.

Fuck, what if we had pups, and I hurt one of them? Or even just traumatized them by going berserk if I thought one of them was threatened?

I still remembered how traumatized my younger brothers had been when I nearly killed our dad.

Summer looked the way they had. Pale. Horrified.

She might get over it, now free of her ex, but I didn't want to see her look at me like this again, which she would. Plus, I didn't want my own pups looking at me in the same fearful way. I didn't want to put my family in the position of knowing I was a danger. I was like a vicious guard dog who couldn't be trusted not to go savage. That I *would* go savage at any time.

I took a step back to give her space. Stepped on broken glass but didn't feel it. Didn't feel how cold the room was now. "Summer, I'm sorry. Fuck. I didn't mean to scare you."

She was in shock. She didn't seem able to speak. She just kept staring at me with those beautiful wide blue eyes.

I stumbled back some more, toward the door, my hands raised. When I saw they were covered in blood, I dropped them to my sides. "I'm sorry. I'm too danger-ous. I...I could've hurt you. If we had pups and I did this–" A tight band closed around my throat. "This isn't going to work." The door was broken so I pushed it open.

"What?" Her voice sounded wispy. Confusion flickered over her expression.

"I'll stay out of your life. You don't deserve this kind of mess. I'm sorry." I pushed Kyle and Levi out of the way, shifted, and ran out into the snow.

30

SUMMER

"Wait! Boone!" I called after the giant white and silver wolf.

The wolf that was twice the size of a normal animal and probably three times as ferocious. That was my mate.

I knew Boone was a shifter, but until he actually shifted in real life before me, it wasn't completely real. Now it was.

He'd leapt and *shattered the motel window*. Glass was everywhere. Snow was blowing in.

He'd broken Marty's neck at the same time he ripped out his throat. Marty was dead, sprawled on the ugly carpet.

I'd known when the animal crashed through the window, it had to be Boone, but I was still in shock from what I'd seen. From witnessing a violent death.

Now, I registered Boone's loss like I'd just lost a limb. I wanted him in here, holding me. Talking through what happened. Reassuring me that everything was going to be okay.

Instead, he'd left. Literally ran out.

And before he'd gone, he'd made it sound final.

I'll stay out of your life.

My entire body shook, and tears flooded down my cheeks. How could he say that?

Except I knew what he was thinking. Boone had a deep belief that he was a danger to the people he loved. He'd fought with and badly hurt his father when he was just sixteen. Teens were dramatic as fuck anyway, so traumas that happened during those years shape beliefs about everything. Left scars that didn't heal.

Boone's definitely hadn't healed. Then he'd said he'd hurt that stalker in New York years later. That was why he'd put himself into self-imposed isolation up on the mountain.

We'd talked about it. I thought he'd been able to move past it, but I guessed I was wrong.

Damn him! How dare he walk out on me, especially at a time like this?

The tears wouldn't stop. My face crumpled. A sob surged up.

"He left. He fucking left."

The sheriff looked over from where they stood over Marty. I hadn't met either of them before, but I presumed he was one of the wolves since he'd commanded Boone to shift. Maybe the other guy, too, since he'd said it in his presence.

"I'm sorry. Summer?" He stepped over Marty's body and held out his hand. "I'm Levi. I'm Boone's pack brother. This is Kyle–he's Cody's father-in-law."

That meant... Riley's dad. Surely he knew about shifters then.

"Looks like he hit you good," he said. "You need me to call an ambulance or want us to take you to the hospital?"

I reached up, winced when I touched my cheek, then kept right on crying. "It hurts, but nothing's broken," I got out between sniffs.

"I can call Audrey to meet us when we get back to town. You met the doc already?"

I nodded, making my head throb.

Knowing they were on my side helped. I definitely had PTSD from Marty and his cop friends who I knew wouldn't have helped me if I ever called 9-1-1 when he got violent.

"Boone shouldn't have run off," Levi said, rubbing

the back of his neck. "He, uh, has issues from when he was young."

That just made me cry harder. I was crying for Boone. Crying for the loss of Boone.

"I know," I sniffed. "His dad. That's no excuse to walk out on me when I need him most."

Both Levi and Kyle winced. "Yeah, that was bad. But he'll be back once he has his head on straight. If not, I'll kick some sense into him."

The tears kept streaming down my face. I was sure it was part release from getting kidnapped and beaten, but all of my focus went into grief over Boone.

He left me.

Left me.

How *could* he? After all those times he said *mine?*

I shivered from the cold pouring in through the broken window and the grotesque scene on the floor.

"Shit. Glad you called, Levi. Also got a call from Cody. How'd you find them?"

All three of us turned at the voice.

There in the doorway was Rob Wolf, and beside him, Willow, his wife. They were staring down at Marty's lifeless body.

"We had an APB out on the rental car, and Cody told us which direction to head. Luckily, it was easy to spot from the highway."

Rob's gaze shifted to me. When he took in the

disaster that probably was my face, his jaw clenched. "You okay?"

I nodded.

"Boone?" he asked.

"G–g...one," I stuttered.

"He thinks he's a danger to his mate," Kyle said. He definitely was up on the whole wolf-thing.

Rob rubbed his face and sighed. "Fuck."

Willow came over, pulled me in for a hug. I hugged her back although it wasn't the best one I'd ever given. She remained beside me.

"He's um, my ex, well, my husband is a cop. What are we going to do?" I asked.

"You're gonna go with Willow now," Rob said. "She'll bring you home and have Audrey stop by to look at your injuries." He looked down at Marty, set his hands on his hips. "This? We'll take care of this. Shifter laws apply here."

I flicked my gaze to Levi, the sheriff, who nodded.

Human law enforcement or shifter justice? Maybe he was both.

"I don't know how I'd explain this to the police anyway," I said. "The LAPD didn't believe me when he was literally abusing me, and this truth is pretty unbelievable."

Levi smiled. "Then it's a good thing I'm the law around here, isn't it?"

It was over with Marty. It was over *for* Marty. I didn't have to worry about him any longer. I was free.

Except I was without Boone.

I'd thought I wanted to be rid of Marty and to move on with my life. But now, my life was with Boone.

What was I going to do without him?

31

BOONE

I RACED through the snow blindly.

My paws were frozen and bloodied from hitting unseen rocks. I didn't want to stop moving–couldn't stop moving.

I ran like I was being chased.

And maybe I was. By the image of my frightened mate. By the monster that I'd become–a killer.

The snowfall tapered off as I climbed a peak. I was exhausted, even in my wolf form. I'd run full out for miles to get Summer then flat out once again to get away from her once I knew she was safe with Levi.

I rested upon a rise, looking out over the entire

valley. With my thick fur, I wasn't cold. I could survive the coldest of winters without shelter.

Where should I go? What should I do?

Fuck.

All I wanted to do was keep on running. See if I could outpace the grief and disappointment I felt right now in myself.

Fate, I'd struggled for years with what I'd done to my father. I'd even left the pack, staying gone for almost eight years because of it. Then, I only came back because of what I did to Sara's stalker. Summer had helped me come to terms with the fact that he'd deserved to be taken out because who knew what he would have done to Sara, but still, I'd lost control. I could've killed him and Sara.

But those incidents? Those were nothing, *nothing,* in comparison to what I just did.

I killed a man. I killed Summer's husband. She was trying to divorce him, but he was still legally her spouse. And I ripped his throat out in front of her.

No control. Nothing.

Just... a gruesome death.

The way Summer looked at me with horror... I sat back on my haunches and howled at the sky, where the clouds were starting to break. The moon was behind them somewhere.

Summer. Fuck.

It killed me to be away from her. She'd been hurt and scared. And I left her alone in the middle of that chaos. But I'd had to leave because I was the one who'd scared her.

But how was I to live without my mate?

She was marked and claimed. She was mine.

I wasn't going to force her to stick with me. I didn't want her trapped the way she'd been with Marty. It would be so much worse because of the damage I could inflict. She saw how lethal I was. How reckless. How wild.

I was worse than her husband.

I didn't deserve her.

32

SUMMER

Boone didn't come back last night. Rand and Natalie were sure he would. They'd thought he just needed to think things through, and then he'd show up at my apartment with his tail between his legs. I didn't know—maybe they meant literally since he was in wolf form when he left. I'd feared they were wrong because I knew Boone.

He'd stayed away from his pack and his family for years after getting violent with his dad. He'd banished himself to a cabin on the mountain after he hurt that guy in New York.

We'd called Roy and Ace last night to fill them in on what happened and ask if they'd seen Boone. They hadn't, but Ace went over to his cabin to see if there were any signs of him. There hadn't been.

I'd called Cody last night to see if Boone's truck was still in the saloon parking lot, and it was. Wherever Boone was, he was probably still in wolf form.

I sent off another text to Ace:

> Any word or signs from Boone?

His reply came immediately:

> No. I spent the night at his place just in case he came back, but he's not here. Roy said he hasn't shown up over there, either.

Tears speared my eyes.

Damn him!

I threw the covers back and swung my legs over the side of the bed. I felt so heavy. My face throbbed, making my skull ache, too. Marty had hit me good, but the ache in my cheek didn't match the ache in my heart.

Audrey had checked me out last night and had me take ibuprofen and put arnica on the bruise to prevent swelling, but I guessed they'd worn off because it hurt like hell now.

I padded to the bathroom and looked in the mirror.

Whoa. Was that me? It wasn't the bruise that threw me off. It was the bleakness of my expression. I didn't remember ever looking or feeling this bereft, even in the middle of figuring out if I could escape my marriage to Marty.

It seemed obvious why. Boone had quickly become everything to me. So much more than Marty. More than anyone in my life. What we had was a deep soul connection. Or a fated connection, I guessed he would say.

No wonder it felt like my heart had been ripped from my chest and put in the blender.

And suddenly, it became clear. I'd been feeling sorry for myself. Angry with Boone for abandoning me when I needed him most, but that wasn't true.

He needed *me* right now.

He *had* been there when I needed him most. Now, it was my turn to be strong. For *him*.

He was staying away out of his love and protection for me. Because he was functioning under the faulty assumption that he wasn't safe for me.

Oh Boone.

I'm too dangerous. I... I could've hurt you. If we had pups, and I did this...

God, I felt awful for him. My heart hurt because I realized how much he must be hurting. Thinking the worst.

Boone had rescued me, as I'd known with all certainty he would. He'd rescued me, and my reaction had been shock and fear. That triggered his deepest wound. His fear of harming me drove him away and kept him there.

I had to figure out how to get him back. How to reassure him that I wasn't afraid of him. That I knew all the way to my bones that he'd never hurt me or... our pups.

Pups. What an adorable word.

God, I hadn't wanted to have kids before. Or at least not with Marty. I thought that even from the beginning–I'd known on some subconscious level that he'd be a terrible dad.

But Boone would be fucking amazing.

And yeah. I wanted to have his pups.

I took a quick shower and got dressed, suddenly motivated. I had to find Boone. He needed me right now, and I wasn't going to curl up and play victim.

I went down to Rand and Natalie's for coffee and found them in the farmhouse kitchen. Natalie was spreading jelly on a piece of toast. She abandoned it and grabbed a mug for me and reached for the coffee pot.

"Ace spent the night at Boone's place, but he never came back," I announced without even a *good morning.*

Natalie handed me the full cup of coffee, and I poured some cream in. Sighed.

"Cody checked the security cameras of the saloon parking lot and said the truck's still there," Rand reported.

A little relief registered knowing everyone was taking this seriously. I wasn't the only one who cared about Boone.

I blinked back tears. "Where do you think he is? Do you think he got hit by a car or something?"

Rand shook his head. "Definitely not. But even if he did, he'd be okay. He'd heal up fast. Wolf shifters are very hard to kill."

Right. A little more relief trickled through my chest.

"Okay, so he's probably not hurt. He's just... staying away?"

Rand's expression was serious. "It seems so."

"Well, what can we do? How can we find him? I can't just sit here." I couldn't stop the edge of desperation from creeping into my voice.

Rand pulled out his phone. "I'm calling Rob," he said.

Rob. That was good. He was the alpha wolf. He'd know what to do.

At least I hoped he would.

Rand quickly updated Rob then listened. "Okay...

yeah. Sounds good. We'll be right over." He ended the call and looked at me and Natalie.

"We're going to hunt him, wolf style. Rob's sending out an all-pack alert. Natalie has to go to work, but you can wait at Rob's house while we search."

"I'll call in sick," Natalie said, shaking her head. "This is more important." She reached for me, and I fell into her arms, desperately needing the hug.

"Thank you," I choked. "You two have been here for me so much this past year, and it means everything."

"Of course. You're part of the pack." Rand joined, making it a brief group hug. "Now let's go find your man."

33

BOONE

I woke curled up in a snowdrift. My fur and the snowbank made it a warm nest, protected from the cold air and wind.

It was quiet. Only white all around me.

Unfortunately, the stillness and quiet didn't cut the noise in my head.

Last night, I ran for hours without paying attention to where I was going. I pushed my way to the surface of my little nest and shook the snow off my fur.

Where in the fuck was I?

I'd been out of my mind with self-loathing and grief and had run blindly.

I sat on my haunches to survey the landscape. I was up in the mountains, but where? How far had I gone? Animal wolf packs' range could extend a thousand square miles. Shifters didn't usually roam that far. Our human side kept us closer to conventional shelter. There was a fear that if we stayed in wolf form too long, we'd go feral and be unable to shift back to human form.

Maybe that was what I should do. Run straight to Canada, away from all civilization, where no shifters could find me. Or I could do the opposite and stay close and let the shifters find me and put me down. Surely Rob had connected with Johnny to track me and finish me.

That was what they had to do with feral shifters. Not only were we a danger to humans, but if humans ever caught or killed a shifter in wolf form, it could expose our species. That meant feral shifters were a significant danger to our kind. They couldn't be controlled or trusted.

Like me.

Yeah. My choices were either to stay on the run or allow myself to be hunted and killed.

I put my snout in the snow and licked it to slake my thirst. I still had the nasty taste of blood and flesh in my mouth, and I was sure my muzzle was coated in it.

The memory of what I'd done slammed back into my head. That asshole hitting my mate. Looming over her as she was tied to the fucking foot of the bed. Summer's wide eyes after I'd killed him. How she'd scooted away in fear.

Fuck.

Pain ripped through me.

I would never see her again.

My beautiful, sweet mate.

How would I survive that?

I already knew the answer–I wouldn't. I wouldn't go moon mad because I'd marked her, but my wolf would go crazy just the same. I couldn't live without my mate. Couldn't breathe knowing I'd never get to touch her again. To make love to her. To hear her scream my name–

Fuck. I had to stop this anguish.

I couldn't think about Summer. My stomach roiled. I'd have to hunt something to eat soon, but I had no interest.

I had no interest in anything.

I lifted my snout to the sky and howled.

Somewhere, at least a mile away, I heard another wolf howl back. Distant, but recognizable.

My fur raised, instantly recognizing the sound. My alpha.

Shit. So I was still on pack land. I should've known I'd end up back here. My wolf had stuck to the familiar. Well, I guessed my wolf made the choice for me–I'd let myself be put down. Maybe then I'd finally get some peace.

I'd rather it was my own pack members, anyway.

Another howl sounded from the same direction, and I stood, feeling forcefully compelled to go to him.

I howled again, in answer and started running in the direction of the other wolves.

It took twenty minutes, maybe more, over rocky and snow covered terrain before I found them–or maybe they found me through our call and answer system of howling.

We met in a saddle at the top of the mountain behind Rob's house. I knew my wolf pack. Recognized their wolves. Rob, my alpha. Willow, his luna. Levi, Johnny, Clint, Rand, Colton, Boyd and–fuck. Ace and Roy were here, too.

I wished to fate they weren't. I didn't want them to have to watch their brother die at the jaws of their alpha.

Levi trotted through the snow to stand beside me, then Rob jerked his head around and turned and headed in the direction from where he'd come. The others turned as well. I knew what this meant, what was required. I had to follow. I didn't have any choice, especially with Levi at my side. With Johnny here, maybe he'd mete out shifter justice quickly. I killed someone in the human world. I would finally get what I deserved.

34

SUMMER

MARINA SET a cookie sheet of fresh-baked peanut butter chocolate chip cookies she'd just pulled from the oven on the huge farm table in Rob's kitchen to cool, but I had zero interest in the delicious treat.

I paced the length of the large kitchen, my socks slippery on the wood floor.

"Rob and the others have gone after him," Marina said. "They'll find him."

I nodded, but her words, meant to be reassuring, did nothing to stop the tight contraction of muscles up under my ribs.

Just then, Natalie's phone buzzed with a text. I spun to face her, wringing my hands.

"It's Rand," she said, looking at it.

I lunged to look over her shoulder.

We found him. Rob brought him to the pack cabin to discuss things.

"Discuss things?" I asked. "What does he mean by that?"

Natalie and Marina shared a look.

"What?" I demanded. My heart was in my throat. I didn't like that look.

"Well, I don't know exactly. But it sounds like this is a pack thing. They have to take care of it in a specific way," Natalie explained.

"It?" I narrowed my eyes, not liking how that sounded. "What do you mean by *a specific way*?"

Neither woman said anything, and I wanted to strangle them both.

"What do you mean a specific way?" I demanded again.

"No, it's probably nothing," Natalie said, but I noticed a crease between her brows.

"*What's* nothing?"

"It's just that Boone's acting kind of irrationally. I mean, Rob would have to see if he really is too dangerous. Or if he's gone feral."

"Feral? What do you mean?"

"Sometimes wolves go feral. Like they stay in wolf

form and don't want to change back. When that happens..."

Alarm bells clanged. Fear shot through me–more fear than I'd felt yesterday for my own safety. So much more. My face was sore, but I'd been icing it and taking the ibuprofen. It was fine. Why would I care about that when Boone might be considered *feral*?

"What?"

"Well, he might have to be put down."

What? PUT DOWN?

"The hell he will," I snarled. "Where are they? Take me to that cabin right now," I demanded, heading toward the back door where I'd set my boots.

"We should just wait," Natalie said, sitting an arm on my shoulder. As if that would stop me. "They'll come back here after Alpha has sorted things out."

I shook my head. "No. No way. I'm not letting anyone touch Boone. He's my mate." Tears filled my eyes. "They can't hurt him! I love him, and Rob needs to know that he did what he did to Marty to protect me."

"I definitely think Rob understands that," Marina said gently, coming to stand in front of me. "It would just be a matter of whether he's too far gone now."

Too far gone?

A tear spilled down my face. There was no way he was too far gone. He couldn't be.

And even if he were, I would bring him back. I wouldn't let him go feral. I wouldn't. He was never too far gone for me.

I turned to Natalie and narrowed my eyes. "Either take me up to that cabin so I can talk to Rob, or I'm stealing your truck."

"Whoa, slow down," Marina said, hand raised.

"Now!" I snapped, setting my hands on my hips.

I knew it was no way to talk to my friends, but my heart was in my throat. I needed to be the one to talk to Boone. To get him to come back to me. To all of us. I didn't trust any of them to do it.

Both women started at my exclamation.

"Okay," Natalie said. "Okay. We'll drive up there."

35

BOONE

ROB LED us through the snow to the pack cabin up on the mountain. The one that we used as home base for the full moon runs, pack meetings, and other events.

So he wanted to talk before he decided my fate. Fine.

We stepped inside through the large dog-door as wolves then shifted. Without saying a word, everyone pulled their spare clothes from their cubbies in the mudroom.

"For fuck's sake, Boone," Roy said as we got dressed, accusation heavy in his voice. "You can't bail–"

Rob made a low growling sound in his throat, and

Roy shut up. This was Rob's show. He was alpha. He'd be handling the justice tonight.

No one tried to talk after that.

When we stepped into the open meeting hall, Rob growled, "Me and Boone. The rest of you wait out there."

"Yes, Alpha," the pack members murmured as they filed back out.

I drew in a long breath. It pained my lungs after being out in the cold. I was in a pair of old sweats and a navy flannel. I hadn't gotten around to putting on the socks or shoes I kept saved here.

Rob stared at me, his gaze dark and heavy. "Summer's ex, Marty. He's taken care of. Levi and Kyle will handle any human issues that arise, especially since he was a cop, but nothing should come up."

I didn't know what that meant exactly. He was being vague intentionally. If he wanted me to know more, he'd have said. So I let it go because I knew Marty would never hurt Summer again.

Yet that wasn't why he called me in here to talk with me alone. It was just a warm-up, a reminder of what I'd done and how the pack had to take care of my mistake. The heaviness of being me descended like a lead blanket on my shoulders. I should apologize. Maybe beg for my life.

Instead, what tumbled out was the apology I'd never offered him. The one from fifteen years ago.

"I never wanted your place as Alpha," I admitted.

Rob's brows rose. It was obviously not the conversation he thought we'd be having.

"My dad wanted me to challenge you," I continued. "I know you probably knew that. We fought, and I left. I don't know why I never came clean with you."

Rob rubbed the back of his neck. "Fuck, Boone, has that been eating at you all these years?"

I stared at him in a world of misery. I was suddenly sixteen again–the agony of being me so large it crushed me. I cleared my throat before I continued. "I didn't want you to banish my family. We needed this pack–desperately." I raised my hand and pointed in the direction of the other room where the others waited. "My brothers did. Your parents were everything after our mom died. And then–"

"Hang on, Boone." Rob held up a hand to halt my stilted stream of words. "If you think you owe me an apology, you're out of your goddamn mind. Yeah, I knew. I mean, I figured. You were gone, and your father looked like hell for a few weeks while he healed. He was also a grumpy asshole. I figured when Ace tried to challenge me, but for sure when he tried to force Roy into fighting me for the job a few years later. Do you think I ever blamed *you* for that?"

I ran my fingers through my hair. I wasn't even in the state at that time and had only heard of what happened long after. "Well, you might've seen me as a threat."

"Is that why you stayed away all those years?" Rob sounded incredulous. "In New York City of all fucking places?"

I shrugged. "Yeah, I mean partly. Also, because the fight with my dad was a relationship ender. I nearly killed him."

Rob didn't seem surprised. All I saw was understanding in his expression. "That must've scared you."

Somehow, in our world of alpha male pack life, I'd never expected that kind of straight-shooting. Or compassion. Our dad sure as hell never talked about or validated anyone's feelings. Especially a male being *scared.*

My nose burned. "Yeah. Well, it scared Roy and Ace. So I figured it was better for everyone if I stayed away."

Rob took a step closer to me and dropped a hand on my shoulder. "Boone, I owe *you* an apology. I should've called you when you were in New York. Or visited. I figured something had gone down with your dad, especially because your brothers seemed like they were covering something up, but I was, uh, trying to figure out how to deal with my grief over losing our parents at the same time I learned how to lead a pack."

My eyes burned. "Yeah, of course you were. I never expected you to reach out."

"Well, I should have," he replied. "And I'm sorry. Because maybe if you'd known I never blamed you for any of it, you wouldn't have stayed away."

He was sorry?

"I stayed away because I'm dangerous." My voice sounded like it had been cut by blades.

I heard the sound of a truck pulling up outside. Some more pack members joining us, perhaps.

Rob shook his head. "You're not dangerous, Boone. You're my cousin, which makes you an alpha wolf. You're protective as hell, as you're supposed to be. It's in our blood."

I stared at him. I wanted to believe what he was saying, but the evidence didn't back it up. I always went too far. I fucked things up.

"Have you ever hurt someone who didn't have it coming, Boone?" he asked.

I was sweating, the conflict within me feeling like bumper cars colliding in my brain. "I...I don't know."

Rob shook his head. "*I* know. You haven't. Summer's ex? He would have eventually killed her. I saw what he'd done to her already. Pack justice would have sentenced him to death. You're not a danger,

Boone. You're just alpha as fuck. We come from a long blood line of alpha wolves."

The door burst open and–oh fate! My entire body lit up, magnetized to the female who flew through it. Summer came rushing in.

"Nobody's touching my mate!" she shouted and then saw me.

Her mate. She was claiming me. She still wanted me, even after what I'd done.

Before I knew what was happening, Summer's arms flew around my waist, and she hugged me tight.

"Baby," I said softly, setting my hand on her hair. It was a whispered prayer. A benediction. A sacred vow.

Summer was here. My wolf in me was soothed.

Fate, I'd nearly died without her. Or at least I'd wanted to. Now it felt like I'd suddenly woken up from a coma.

I was alive again. She was my reason to live and breathe. She was my sunshine. My music. My connection with other humans.

She turned to glare at Rob. "He's *safe*," she snarled, savagery in her voice. She even poked his chest once. "Nobody's putting him down. He would never, *ever* hurt anyone who didn't deserve it."

Rob's lips quirked in a small smile. "You know, Summer, that's what I was just telling him."

"You were?" She adjusted her tone and dropped

her arm. "Well, good. Thank you." She lifted her face to me and frowned. "Boone, don't *ever* run away like that again."

My heart grew wings that started to flap.

I cradled her beautiful face in my hands. Her cheek was swollen and cut, which killed me. "I won't," I promised. "I'm sorry, baby. I..."

I realized Rob had stepped out to give us some privacy.

"I lost control," I explained. "I scared you, and I'll never forgive myself for–"

"No." Summer shook her head. She spoke the word firmly enough to shut me up. "You weren't out of control. You were perfectly safe with me. You did everything you needed to protect me and save me from Marty, and I absolutely love you for it." Her eyes brimmed with tears. "So don't you *dare* blame yourself for anything."

Her fierceness wrung a small smile from me.

My beautiful mate showed up to fight for me. She faced down an alpha wolf. For me. She claimed me. She wasn't afraid.

"But you ran when I still needed you," she said. "And that hurt."

I ran a hand through my messy hair. "Fuck, Summer. I'm so sorry. I just... I thought you'd be safer without me."

She shook her head. "No. I *need* you, Boone. I don't want to be without you. Not ever again." Her eyes shone with tears. She poked me in the chest and screwed her face up to look stern. "You are my mate. So don't run off ever again. That's a rule."

I let out a relieved chuckle. It seemed crazy that I could go from hating myself to floating six inches off the ground in the span of a few minutes, but I had. Rob didn't hate me. Hell, he apologized to me and not the other way around.

Summer needed me. She didn't want to be free of me. She wasn't afraid of me. I thought I'd fucked up by killing her ex, but my actual fuck-up was leaving my mate. It suddenly felt crystal clear.

"I... I won't leave you ever again. I promise."

The door swung open, and Roy stomped in, followed by Ace.

"I hope you punched him in the teeth for running off," he growled at Summer.

She drew up tall—all five foot three of her—and angled her body like she was going to protect me. "No, I didn't. He's suffered enough. And you guys need to work your past shit out right now," she commanded.

My lips quirked some more. My mate was fierce when she wanted to be, and I fucking loved it.

She put her hands on her hips and told them every-thing I had yet to say to them. "Boone is racked with guilt over abandoning you two, but he also felt like it was the best thing to do to preserve family harmony. He thought he was too dangerous to stay and that he traumatized you by fighting your dad in front of you."

I nearly dropped to the floor with the honor of being so well understood. Summer had just met me not two weeks ago, yet it felt like she really saw me. Like she knew me better than I even knew myself.

I was also ashamed that it had taken me all these years to just get this shit out on the table–with both Rob and my brothers. How many years had we gone without talking about any of it? Just avoiding it all?

"Traumatized us? Fuck no. You leaving was the only trauma we experienced," Ace said. "We needed you, Boone. Dad was a fucking asshole, and you bailed. Just like you bailed on your mate when she needed you."

My throat closed with a lump. "I'm sorry," I choked, looking from Ace to Roy to Summer. "I fucked up."

"Thank you." Summer accepted my apology with the same grace she did everything. "We *need* you fierce. We need you dangerous. Stop being afraid of who you are and trying to shield the world from it. You're exactly what you're supposed to be–a danger to anyone who fucks with the people you love."

It was the same thing Rob said.

My eyes burned, and I suddenly couldn't breathe. I wrapped my arms around Summer from behind, holding on to my lifeline.

"She's right, man," Roy said, giving me a smile. "No one here is afraid you're a danger but you. So stop holing up like a hermit and get back to living. You have a mate now. A mate who's getting famous." Roy winked at Summer, who smiled back.

I kissed the top of her head. My chest ached from my heart swelling so damn big. The people I loved most in the world also cared for each other. It was a beauty I never thought I'd experience.

"Yeah," Ace said. "You're probably going to have to tour the world with her, so get used to being around people."

Summer's smile grew even broader. "I don't know about that."

"I do," I said with total certainty. "Recording deal, tour, fandemonium. That's what's coming for you, my beautiful woman."

"And you were going to abandon *that*?" Roy spread his palm and shook it in Summer's direction for emphasis.

"I'm not a *that*." She turned in my arms and looked up at me. "And he's not abandoning me ever again. Right?"

"*Never*," I swore. "That's the rule. I'm sorry. I owe each of you an apology."

"Bring it in, man." Roy clasped my hand in a bro-grip and pulled me in for a thump on the back.

Ace did the same. "Yeah, man. We love you. Stop being a giant turd."

Summer reclaimed her position in my arms and squeezed me. "Let's go home."

Home.

I didn't know which home Summer meant, but it didn't matter to me. Home was wherever she was. And yeah, I'd follow her to the ends of the fucking earth. At least that was clear now that I'd unwedged my head from my ass.

I swung her up into my arms. "Home sounds like exactly where I need to be, baby."

36

SUMMER

"I'M SORRY, BABY." Boone lowered my feet to the floor in his cabin. Ace and Roy had dropped us off at Boone's cabin, and he carried me inside. All the others had headed to their homes as well.

He cradled my cheek, lowering his head to give me a slow, gentle kiss. "I should've been with you last night. I should've held you in my arms and comforted you after what happened."

I didn't want him to feel any more guilty than he already did, but it was a relief to hear that he under-stood that he'd hurt me. It hopefully meant he wouldn't withdraw again. That there wouldn't be a next time in his pattern of having a violent incident and taking off.

"I felt abandoned," I admitted because owning my feelings was part of a healthy relationship. Or so I'd learned from the books I'd read trying to fix a doomed marriage. "I was pretty mad at first."

He eyed my bruise, his brows lowered. "I should've been the guy holding ice to your face."

"I wish you had," I admitted. "But when you hadn't returned this morning, I realized I was making this about me when I was the one who was safe at home. You were the one who was in danger and suffering. So I realized you needed me as much as I needed you."

Boone blinked rapidly, his eyes turning red. "I did need you. I won't make it without you." Then he looked slightly alarmed, like he'd said the wrong thing. "I mean, that doesn't mean you're stuck–"

I put my fingertips over his lips. "Don't. Don't police yourself with me anymore. I know at first I freaked out. I was comparing everything you did and said to Marty, and some things seemed like red flags, but I was dead wrong." I started to unbutton his flannel shirt. "I want you to know I'm not afraid of you. I don't think you're too possessive. I have zero reservations about you, Boone. About us." I slid his shirt down over his shoulders, baring his gorgeous, sculpted chest, heavily dusted with soft brown curls. I let my palms wander over his muscles, stroking him with appreciation.

He pulled my sweater off over my head and tossed it onto the floor.

I unbuttoned his jeans. "I didn't know about fate before, but now I believe, too. We're together because we were meant to be. You and me."

This time when he kissed me, he wasn't gentle. He was ferocious. His mouth devoured mine, lips crashing down, tongue sweeping into my mouth. He gripped the back of my head to hold me in place for the onslaught, showing me how he felt.

"I love you, Boone," I said when he let me up for a breath.

"Fuck, Summer. I love you so fucking much." He returned to the frenzied kissing, squeezing my ass, and walking me backward until my legs hit the bed, and we tumbled down on top of it. He braced one arm beside my head, holding his weight above me, so he didn't crush me when we fell.

"I love *you* so fucking much," I countered.

A wicked expression crept over his face. "So, you're saying I don't have to hold back anymore?"

My brows rose. "You were holding back?"

"Oh yeah, baby. I was holding *way* back." He rose to his knees and yanked my yoga pants and panties down my legs. "You're about to find out what a dominant alpha wolf sounds like in bed."

My pussy clenched, a shudder of lust tearing through me. "Yes, please."

He stared down at my mostly-naked body with glittering eyes. "Mine."

His. Yes, I liked how that sounded. I wasn't scared of it any longer. In fact, I craved it. My body was perfectly tuned to him. To his touch. His voice. His presence. Just like he was made for me. I was his, and he was mine.

He shoved his sweats down his hips and kicked them off. "I'm gonna need to see those perfect tits of yours. *Bra off*." There was a command in his voice that sent an absolute thrill through my body.

I knew it was a game. That I was perfectly safe. That he'd never hurt me. And that made his dominance sexy as hell. I'd been in a situation where I was scared of my partner. I knew I never would be again.

I slid my bra straps down my shoulders and held Boone's gaze as I unhooked my bra. Then I held the garment in place, covering my breasts, testing him.

He flicked his brows as he climbed over me on all fours. His cock was hard for me, brushing my belly. "I said, *bra off*, baby. I need to see if those sweet nipples are hard and tight for me yet, or if you need me to run my tongue around them and suck them until they're good and stiff."

Oh God. My pussy clenched again. I had no idea Boone was a master at dirty talk.

I'd been *missing out*.

I slowly lowered the fabric of the bra, revealing my nipples, which were definitely already hard and tight. Still, I looked down then back at him and said, "Maybe they need a little more coaxing."

Boone's lips curved into a satisfied smirk as he lowered his head. He flicked his tongue just once over my right nipple. Then once over my left. Then he blew on them, so the moisture cooled and dried, causing a fresh sensation.

I arched up in appreciation. "More."

Boone tilted his head, like he was considering whether to comply with my request. "Who do these gorgeous tits belong to?"

My brain stuttered with a defensive response, but then I remembered it was a game. A very delicious game. "You."

His smile was feral. "That's right, baby. This body is mine. Mine to pleasure." He cupped my right breast, his thick fingers molding around the side and angled it toward his mouth. This time he took my nipple into his mouth, sucking hard.

I cried out, feeling the answering tug between my legs. "Oh, God."

"You can call me a god." I loved hearing him sound smug. "I *am* gonna give you a transcendental experience."

I moaned when he returned his mouth to my nipple and sucked again then released the suction and lightly grazed the erect tip with his teeth.

He sat up, straddling my waist, and stroked both hands around my breasts, then down my sides. He lowered his lips to kiss along my jaw and down the side of my neck.

He was taking too long. I needed him inside of me. I was already desperate.

"Please. Fuck me, Boone."

He smiled but continued his kisses interspersed with flicks of his tongue. Across my collarbone. Between my breasts. Down the soft plane of my stomach. "Greedy little thing, aren't you?"

"Yes," I moaned.

"You think you're ready for my cock?"

"I am."

"Hmm. Let's see." He reached his fingers between my legs at the same time he kissed lower, over my mons, to the apex of my labia. The pads of his fingers dipped into my dripping entrance. "Mmm. Yes, you're making a lot of that sweet honey for me, aren't you, beautiful?"

I was losing the ability to speak or think coherent thoughts. All I could do was let out a warbling sigh of pleasure.

Boone shoved two fingers up inside me at the same time his tongue delved between my nether lips, parting them.

I cried out. "Oh! Oh...."

He stroked my inner wall with the tips of his fingers, stimulating what must be my G-spot.

"Boone!" If I sounded alarmed, it was only because it was almost *too* much pleasure. Too much stimulation. I needed something more. Something to help me release the rapidly-building tension.

"Please... Boone!"

Boone found my clit–where all those nerves from my G-spot connected and sucked it.

I screamed, an orgasm ripping through me. "Oh my God! Oh my God!" I definitely sounded alarmed. It was so much. Too intense. I screamed–literally screamed–a high-pitched keening cry–for several long seconds until I finished.

Then I fell back on the bed, panting like I'd just been chased for a mile by a bear.

"Oh my God, Boone," I said, trying to catch my breath. "What are you doing to me?"

He rolled me over and gave my ass a slap. In my

delirious state, it registered as pure pleasure. "I'm satis-fying my mate." He slapped the other cheek. "This is my job, baby. Pleasuring you is my favorite thing in the whole fucking world."

Oh my God. He spanked me!

An after-quake rolled through me–a whole body shiver with a clenching of my internal muscles.

"Ohhhhh," I moaned, already wrung out from what I assumed was just the foreplay.

"Now, are you gonna be a good girl and take my cock?" Boone nudged my thighs wider, shifting to kneel between them instead of on the outside of them.

"Mmm."

Boone leaned over and lightly bit my shoulder. "Hmm?" His cock nudged my entrance, and I arched my back to welcome him. "You ready to get plowed?"

Oh, *damn.*

My pussy squeezed again. I was dizzy with lust. This man could dirty talk like no other. He was making me come just with his words.

"Uh huh," I whimpered. I definitely needed to feel him inside me. Fingers were no substitute for the real thing, in my opinion.

He slid in easily, going slowly, so I had time to adjust to his size.

"Yummm," I murmured.

Boone chuckled. "Is that yummy to you, baby?" He

eased out and pushed in again. "You like taking it from behind?"

"Yessss," I moaned.

"Maybe you'd like it even better with a pillow under your hips." He wrapped his huge arm around my waist and lifted them to make room for a pillow.

He was right. I did like it better. The angle allowed him to get even deeper.

I moaned in rhythm with his strokes, spreading my legs even wider, lifting my ass higher.

"Yeah, you like that. You like it when I get deep, don't you, baby?"

"Yes," I agreed.

"I'm gonna fuck you hard. Is that what you want?"

He didn't have to ask for my consent. I already knew with total certainty that Boone would stop immediately if something hurt me. He would take care of me. I could trust him with my body, and now that we'd worked through his beliefs about being danger-ous–my heart.

Still, I gave him the consent he desired. "I want it." Later we could talk about my blanket consent, even for pretend non-consent. I was totally down with playing rough with him because he was the man who would kill or die for me.

He growled, gripping my shoulder at the nape to hold me in place as he fucked me hard. The bed bounced and banged against the wall. I squealed my pleasure. Boone's movements grew jerky.

"Fuck, baby. I'm going to come already. I can't hold back."

"Yes!" I cried. "Come!"

He picked up more speed, his loins slapping my ass, the slick sounds of our love-making echoing in the small cabin.

"You're taking my cock like a good girl. Such a good girl…"

I didn't know I had a praise kink, but I loved hearing his adulation.

"Fuck, baby. Fuck. Put your hands on the head-board. Spread those legs wider. Give me that sweet ass. That's right." He pounded into me, and I lost my breath.

Oh. My. *Gawd.* I was surprised the bed hadn't burst into flames.

"I'm coming. You with me?"

"Yes!" I was definitely a vaginal penetration kind of orgasm girl. I liked having my clit touched, but I didn't need it to go off.

Boone slammed in, and I swear I could feel the heat of his cum filling me. I squeezed around his dick, intentionally at first, then my body got the message, and I orgasmed, hard. The room spun. I felt light headed.

Boone groaned, still releasing. His fingers reached under my hips and found my clit, and I convulsed again, coming for the third time. "That's my good girl," he purred. "I'm gonna keep you coming day and night."

EPILOGUE

SUMMER

"I can't believe this is happening." I squeezed Boone's hand, looking up at the towering glass-windowed building that housed Sara's music recording company. I was from LA and used to crowds, but there was something different about New York. Taller. So crowded. Loud. Thrilling, but it also made me crave our quiet, peaceful cabin in the woods.

It was spring, and Boone and I were in Manhattan to sign the contract my lawyer, Selena Jenkins, had negotiated. She was a shifter and part of the Wolf pack, but also handled human legal matters. For her, mine was a fun one. It wasn't every day someone received a music deal!

Boone had booked a recording studio for me in Missoula, and I'd recorded my demo and sent it off to Sara as requested. She'd followed up almost immediately with a sample contract.

It seemed too easy. Too good to be true.

But that's how my relationship with Boone seemed, too.

I'd stopped looking for red flags, but it still had taken me the last few months to really believe how good my life had become. To really receive everything Boone wanted to give me. To know that I deserved it, that I was worthy, and I gave it back with the same energy.

He spoiled me with his attention, his kindness, his lovemaking, and his money. It seemed like all he needed in return was for me to let him, but I tried to give back in other ways, too. I was making sure he stayed social, went to pack meetings and runs, and built his community. He and his brothers got along better now, which was amazing, because I loved them, too.

"It's totally happening." Boone opened the door for me, and we entered the building. It was sleek and modern, with fancy marble floors and a lofted ceiling.

I drew in a breath to speak to the guard manning a front desk, telling him that we were there to see Sara.

"I'm so nervous," I confessed to Boone as we

stepped into the elevator. I gripped his hand, and he gave mine a squeeze.

"Baby, you have nothing to worry about." He leaned down and kissed the top of my head. "The contract has already been negotiated. This is just for ceremony."

He was right. I totally could have e-signed the contract, but he'd suggested we fly out and meet Sara in person. He'd said having a face-to-face would solidify the relationship and make sure she really worked hard to get my music out into the world, not that he doubted she would. They'd known each other a long time and had bonded over a dark situation. I trusted his judgment. Plus, he'd wanted to show me around New York City because I'd never been.

We'd flown in a few days ago, first class–my first time–and were staying at the Waldorf Astoria. Yep, he was spoiling me rotten.

Sara was waiting for us outside the elevators on the twenty-third floor.

"Hi, Summer. Boone."

I expected formality, but despite the sleek pantsuit and heels, Sara treated us like family. She went in for a hug from Boone and gave me the same, along with a brilliant smile.

"It's so wonderful to meet you in person, Summer. I'm really excited to have you on board." She waved us forward. "Come on back–we'll get the papers signed, and then I'm taking you both out to lunch."

She brought us to a conference room with a wall of windows that looked out on Manhattan and a giant, modern glass table that could seat probably twenty-five people. The contract was already laid out with a fancy fountain pen and the sticky arrows pointing at the lines where I needed to sign.

I picked up the pen then remembered what my social media manager–aka, Riley–told me about getting it on video. "Um, would you mind filming it? I want to post the big moment on my social media accounts." I took out my phone and thrust it at Sara.

She couldn't help but laugh.

I had learned a lot in the last four months about putting myself out there. Riley had me posting every day–sharing clips of the songs I'd recorded for the demo as well as just random "day in the life of a musician" stuff. I featured Cody's Saloon a lot because I still worked there for fun, and his business had picked up from the fame. It was crazy, but some of my song clips had been reused on other people's posts tens of thousands of times.

Sara wanted to get the professional recordings done next week as soon as the paperwork was final.

"Of course. My assistant will film, too, for our

socials." She indicated the young woman behind her holding a phone.

I smiled at the camera as I signed the paperwork. I was signing! It was happening. Oh my God! I glanced at Boone, who winked.

"Congratulations," Sara said. "You're officially signed. Let's toast the occasion."

Her assistant uncorked a bottle of champagne and poured glasses for the three of us. We stood to clink glasses.

"Here's to you, Summer, and what I know will be a massively successful and abundant career," Sara said. Then she turned to Boone. "And to you, the man who once took a knife for me and saved my life."

The assistant gasped as we clinked our glasses. Clearly, she hadn't known the backstory between her boss and Boone.

Boone looked at me. "No, this is all to you, baby. This is Summer's moment. I don't want to share in your glory. I just want to watch you take off like a rocket ship."

I set my glass down and threw my arms around him. He was so big and warm and strong and... mine. "I could never do this without you."

His arm banded around me, and he pulled me up against him. It was my favorite place in the world to be. Where I felt safe and held and loved. "Yes, you could.

This is all you. But don't worry because I'm not going anywhere. I'll be with you wherever this takes you."

"Aw, you guys are sweet. Why don't you put a ring on it?" Sara demanded.

Boone cleared his throat. "Actually, after lunch I was thinking we could go to Tiffany's to find one."

I gasped. "Are you asking me to marry you?"

He froze, like he realized he'd botched the proposal.

I laughed because I got it–in his mind, and to his kind–we were already more than married. A ring and paperwork were human rituals, not shifter ones, and I never expected them.

"That was not your slickest move, Boone," Sara chided, with a smile to soften it.

Boone dropped to one knee. "How's this?"

"Yes!" I exclaimed to save him from muddling through some speech he hadn't thought to prepare. I knew he loved me. I knew he was committed. I didn't need the slick words or fancy talk. I'd had that before, and it had all been bullshit. What I had with Boone was real. So real I'd stake my life on it.

"Well, that was easy," Sara laughed.

I straddled Boone's knee and carefully sat to kiss his lips. "He's a keeper," I murmured. "Mine," I whispered then kissed him again. He was my man. My mate. My wolf and soon to be my husband.

I was the luckiest woman in the world.

Jump into the Wolf Ranch spinoff series next! Nash from Ruthless will meet his mate in this series… eventually! First, get Untamed in the Two Marks series!
Read Untamed now!

Two Marks Pack Rule: Always mate in pairs.
I caught her scent when I was on enforcer business.
Knew she must be the one.
I brought my alpha back with me. Because our bloodline mates in pairs.
Two males for every she-wolf. The one we're going to spoil and protect.
Carry off to make a home together.
Just as soon as we convince her she belongs to us.

NOTE FROM VANESSA & RENEE

Guess what? We've got some bonus content for you with Summer and Boone. Yup, there's more!

Click here to read more!
or go to this link:
https://vanessavaleauthor.com/v/2pw

GET A FREE VANESSA VALE BOOK!

Join my mailing list to be the first to know of new releases, free books, special prices and other author giveaways.

http://freeromanceread.com

WANT FREE RENEE ROSE BOOKS?

Receive a slew of free Renee Rose books: Go to http://subscribepage.com/alphastemp to sign up for Renee Rose's newsletter and receive free books. In addition to the free stories and bonus material, you will also get special pricing, exclusive previews and news of new releases.

Did you know you can buy direct from Renee Rose? Get signed books, special editions, and heavily discounted bundles. Use this coupon for an additional 10% discount on your entire order - **READER10** or go here https://shop.reneeroseromance.com/discount/READER10

ALSO BY RENEE ROSE

Paranormal

Wolf Ranch Series

Rough

Wild

Feral

Savage

Fierce

Ruthless

Primal

Rugged

Ravenous

Two Marks Series

Untamed

Tempted

Desired

Enticed

Wolf Ridge High Series

Alpha Bully

Alpha Knight

Step Alpha

Alpha King

Alpha Varsity

Bad Boy Alphas Series

Alpha's Temptation

Alpha's Danger

Alpha's Prize

Alpha's Challenge

Alpha's Obsession

Alpha's Desire

Alpha's War

Alpha's Mission

Alpha's Bane

Alpha's Secret

Alpha's Prey

Alpha's Sun

Shifter Ops

Alpha's Moon

Alpha's Vow

Alpha's Revenge

Alpha's Fire

Alpha's Rescue

Alpha's Command

Werewolves of Wall Street

Big Bad Boss: Midnight

Big Bad Boss: Moon Mad

Big Bad Boss: Marked

Big Bad Boss: Mated

Bad Boy Bears Series

Alpha's Claim

Alpha's Mate

Solo Paranormal Romance

Claimed by the Storm

Alpha Doms Series

Dominion (complete collection)

The Alpha's Hunger

The Alpha's Promise

The Alpha's Punishment

The Alpha's Protection

Contemporary

Chicago Bratva

"Prelude" in Black Light: Roulette War

The Director

The Fixer

"Owned" in Black Light: Roulette Rematch

The Enforcer

The Soldier

The Hacker

The Bookie

The Cleaner

The Player

The Gatekeeper

Vegas Underground Mafia Romance

King of Diamonds

Mafia Daddy

Jack of Spades

Ace of Hearts

Joker's Wild

His Queen of Clubs

Dead Man's Hand

Wild Card

Chicago Sin

Den of Sins

Rooted in Sin

Made Men Series

Don't Tease Me

Don't Tempt Me

Don't Make Me

Yacht Kings

Revenge

Alpha Mountain

Hero

Rebel

Warrior

Master Me Series

Her Royal Master

Her Russian Master

Her Marine Master

Yes, Doctor

Her Russian Master

Her Marine Master

Her Fire Master

Her Hollywood Master

Her Stepbrother Master

Double Doms Series

Theirs to Punish

Theirs to Protect

Holiday Feel-Good

Scoring with Santa

Saved

Other Contemporary

Black Light: Valentine Roulette

Black Light: Roulette Redux

Black Light: Celebrity Roulette

Black Light: Roulette War

Black Light: Roulette Rematch

Punishing Portia (written as Darling Adams)

The Professor's Girl

Safe in his Arms

Sci-Fi

Zandian Masters Series

His Human Slave

His Human Prisoner

Training His Human

His Human Rebel

His Human Vessel

His Mate and Master

Zandian Pet

Their Zandian Mate

His Human Possession

Zandian Brides

Night of the Zandians

Bought by the Zandians

Mastered by the Zandians

Zandian Lights

Kept by the Zandian

Claimed by the Zandian

Stolen by the Zandian

Rescued by the Zandian

Other Sci-Fi

The Hand of Vengeance

Her Alien Masters

ALSO BY VANESSA VALE

For the most up-to-date listing of my books:

vanessavalebooks.com

Cowboys of Devil's Ditch

Trig

Colt

Bray

Beau

Cam

Zeb

Shep

Buck

Hayes

The Hitman and the Fixer

Hannah and the Hitman

Fiona and the Fixer

On A Manhunt

Manhunt

Man Candy

Man Cave

Man Sprain

Man Scape

Man Handle

Man Spread

Alpha Mountain

Hero

Rebel

Warrior

Billionaire Ranch

North

South

East

West

Bachelor Auction

Teach Me The Ropes

Hand Me The Reins

Back In The Saddle

Wolf Ranch

Rough

Wild

Feral

Savage

Fierce

Ruthless

Primal

Rugged

Ravenous

Two Marks

Untamed

Tempted

Desired

Enticed

More Than A Cowboy

Strong & Steady

Rough & Ready

Wild Mountain Men

Mountain Darkness

Mountain Delights

Mountain Desire

Mountain Danger

Grade-A Beefcakes

Sir Loin of Beef

T-Bone

Tri-Tip

Porterhouse

Skirt Steak

Big Sky Boyfriends

Misadventures of a Single Mom

Misadventures with the Mistaken Twin

Misadventures with my Billionaire Boss

Misadventures with my Fake Fiancé

Misadventures and Ms. Demeanor

Steele Ranch

Spurred

Wrangled

Tangled

Hitched

Lassoed

Bridgewater County

Ride Me Dirty

Claim Me Hard

Take Me Fast

Hold Me Close

Make Me Yours

Kiss Me Crazy

Mail Order Bride of Slate Springs

A Wanton Woman

A Wild Woman

A Wicked Woman

Bridgewater Brides

Their Runaway Bride

Their Kidnapped Bride

Their Wayward Bride

Their Captivated Bride

Their Treasured Bride

Their Christmas Bride

Their Reluctant Bride

Their Stolen Bride

Their Brazen Bride

Their Rebellious Bride

Their Reckless Bride

Lenox Ranch Cowboys

Cowboys & Kisses

Spurs & Satin

Reins & Ribbons

Brands & Bows

Lassos & Lace

Montana Men

The Lawman

The Cowboy

The Outlaw

The Billion Heirs

Scarred

Flawed

Broken

Standalones

Relentless

Bride Pact

Rough Love

Twice As Delicious

Flirting With The Law

Mistletoe Marriage

Man Candy - A Coloring Book

ABOUT RENEE ROSE

USA TODAY BESTSELLING AUTHOR RENEE ROSE loves a dominant, dirty-talking alpha hero! Readers have devoured over five million copies of her steamy romance with varying levels of kink. Her books have been featured in USA Today's *Happily Ever After* and *Popsugar*. Named Eroticon USA's Next Top Erotic Author in 2013, she has also won *Spunky and Sassy's* Favorite Sci-Fi and Anthology author, *The Romance Reviews* Best Historical Romance, and has hit the *USA Today* list fifteen times with her Bad Boy Alphas, Chicago Bratva, and Wolf Ranch series.

Renee loves to connect with readers!
www.reneeroseromance.com
reneeroseauthor@gmail.com

facebook.com/reneeroseromance

instagram.com/reneeroseromance

bookbub.com/authors/renee-rose

tiktok.com/@reneeroseromance

ABOUT VANESSA VALE

A USA Today bestseller, Vanessa Vale writes tempting romance with unapologetic bad boys who don't just fall in love, they fall hard. Her books have sold over one million copies. She lives in the American West where she's always finding inspiration for her next story.

vanessavaleauthor.com

facebook.com/vanessavaleauthor
instagram.com/vanessa_vale_author
amazon.com/author/vanessavale
bookbub.com/profile/vanessa-vale
tiktok.com/@vanessavaleauthor